The Literature of Cinema

ADVISORY EDITOR: **MARTIN S. DWORKIN**
INSTITUTE OF PHILOSOPHY AND POLITICS OF EDUCATION
TEACHER'S COLLEGE, COLUMBIA UNIVERSITY

THE LITERATURE OF CINEMA presents
a comprehensive selection from the multitude
of writings about cinema, rediscovering ma-
terials on its origins, history, theoretical principles and techniques, aesthetics, economics,
and effects on societies and individuals. Included are works of inherent, lasting merit
and others of primarily historical significance.
These provide essential resources for serious
study and critical enjoyment of the "magic
shadows" that became one of the decisive cultural forces of modern times.

Film Music

Kurt London

ARNO PRESS & THE NEW YORK TIMES

New York • 1970

Reprint Edition 1970 by Arno Press Inc.
Reprinted from a copy in The Museum of Modern Art Library
Library of Congress Catalog Card Number: 70-124016
ISBN 0-405-01622-0
ISBN for complete set: 0-405-01600-X
Manufactured in the United States of America

Film Music

by Kurt London

translated by Eric S. Bensinger

With a foreword by
Constant Lambert

FILM
MUSIC

A Summary of
the Characteristic features
of its History, Aesthetics,
Technique; and possible
Developments

Faber & Faber Ltd
24 Russell Square London

*First Published in July Mcmxxxvi
by Faber and Faber Limited
24 Russell Square London W.C.1
Printed in Great Britain by
R. MacLehose and Company Limited
The University Press Glasgow
All Rights Reserved*

Foreword by Constant Lambert

Few people seem to realise how greatly aesthetic movements, and in particular musical movements, are influenced by outside considerations—social, financial, mechanical. For example, ten to fifteen years ago the most flourishing branch of English music was song writing. I am referring not to the 'song-hit' or 'theme-song', but to the serious setting of serious poetry by composers of the calibre of Warlock, Bax or Moeran. For every fifty songs published then only one is published to-day, and no doubt future historians will search for elaborate philosophical and psychological explanations of this sudden dearth of lyricism. The explanation is simple: owing to the great popularisation of mechanical music people no longer buy sheet music to sing or play in their own homes. Except in a few rare instances the writing of straightforward or 'art' songs has ceased to be a commercial proposition and the average composer has, very sensibly, ceased to write them.

Wireless has not so far compensated the composer by providing him with a new art form though television may possibly do so in the near future. The sound film, on the other hand, opens up fascinating new possibilities of aesthetic and is bound to have a strong influence on the trend of music in this century. It offers the serious composer what has been lacking since the eighteenth century—a reasonable commercial outlet for his activities, comparable to the 'occasional' music which the greatest classical composers did not despise to write. Moreover, it opens up a new life for the composer whose talents are more executive than creative. How familiar is the spectacle of a composer endowed with technical facility and good taste, but with little originality, wasting his time in an effort to be a latter-day Beethoven! Yet these same gifts employed in the film studio might produce results of the utmost value.

Film music should not be despised because it is inevitably more ephemeral and less important than symphonic and operatic music. We do not despise the first-rate poster artist or the first-rate journalist, and the fact that the sound-film has already attracted, in this country alone, composers as eminent as Walton, Bliss, Benjamin, Leigh and Britten is in itself ample justification of the seriousness and thoroughness with which the author has approached his task. In addition to its intrinsic interest as a new craft, writing for films will have the salutary effect of keeping composers in touch with a large audience and its human reactions. It stands to reason that film music must above all be expressive, and the demands made by the film for colourful and expressive music may well be the decisive factor in turning composers away from the drab and fruitless avenues offered by the post-war ideals of 'abstraction' and 'neo-classicism'.

Dr. London's book comes at an opportune moment when the English sound-film is at last attaining artistic and international importance. Apart from its interesting historical survey of film music, from Edison's first experiments to the latest talkie, it gives a very thorough account of present-day microphone technique and its problems which should be invaluable to the cinema composer. But to my mind its most interesting chapters are those dealing with the aesthetic of the sound-film.

The film seems the one form of entertainment whose future is absolutely assured, and it is more than probable that music will play a greater part than speech in its future development. Hence the necessity for composers to study the aesthetic problems of the sound-film as seriously as in the past they studied the aesthetic problems of the opera and the symphony.

CONSTANT LAMBERT

Author's Preface

For many years the film was outlawed by the intelligentsia and so-called good society. It is even now not so very long since it received official recognition, and had the doors of national playhouses opened to it, and saw the rulers of the nations in the audiences attending its *premières*.

But the music which accompanies the film is still struggling for its place in the sun: the film people themselves almost invariably treat it very casually and are not quite clear in their own minds about its importance; musicians take it up more for the sake of fees than for art's sake, and he is a rare exception among them who shows any sympathy for its novel forms; the public, finally, does not trouble overmuch about music, because it almost always fails to understand the cause and effect of film-musical ideas, and is for example only inclined to rate a sound-film theme-song as film music because it happens to be sung or played in a sound-film.

So film music hitherto, with few exceptions, has remained the stepchild of experts and laymen alike.

It is strange enough that not even scientists have probed its highly interesting and for the most part still unsolved problems, on the solution of which the further development of the art of film depends not a little. So it is that, among the thousands of books which have been written all over the world on every aspect of film, so far not one has been solely devoted to film music, except the *Handbook of Film Music*, brought out by Erdmann, Becce and Brav in Berlin, 1927. This deals with directions for cinema conductors playing musical accompaniments to silent films, which soon after became superfluous, when the sound-film superseded the silent version.

It is possible that there are indefinable reasons at the bottom of this very superficial and unmethodical attitude to film music. It sometimes happens that for years some sphere of knowledge languishes in neglect, and then suddenly has the searchlight of interested publicity turned full upon it. All that is needed is the preliminary stimulus: to give that is one of the main motives of this first attempt at a systematic summary of the whole province of film music.

This attempt makes the less claim to be complete, since it is manifestly impossible to examine, in one modest volume, a material scattered in huge quantities over the whole world. Likewise, a few test cases do not afford a proper basis on which to build up the first principles of a science. Finally, and most important of all, it was intended to avoid an all too dry enumeration of names and material. For this book is not meant to make an exclusive appeal to the experts of music and film; it is also intended to stimulate interested amateurs to give the subject the assistance of their ideas and experiments.

A new generation of music listeners is arising. With the changed stratification of society, the methods of artistic performance change also. Opera and concert, in many cases the theatre too, are today only a privilege of a relatively limited circle, which for economic and social reasons will disintegrate more and more. But film, this new art that is not fettered by tradition, is beginning its ascent at the very moment when the 'aristocratic' arts (at least in their public performance) seem to have reached the end of their tether. The film appeals to millions of men of all races and classes. Its influence is growing to gigantic dimensions: for it is already shaping the ideas and tastes of countless numbers. All the more pressing must be the demands made of the cultural consciousness of all those who have anything to do with film production; all the more essential become all the various components affecting the film's characteristic features and lines of development.

Film music is of importance both as an element of film, and of music. As a synthetic art, it has a future

13

before it, of which it is as yet quite impossible to guess all the details and implications. The last chapters of this book are intended to give a short sketch of these ideas, and they point out that this strange combination of picture with sound, which is a revolutionary novelty both in musical theory and in sound technique, calls for extremely zealous and painstaking attention in the future.

If this little work should make its contribution in dragging film music out of the dark shadows of unreal things into the limelight of general discussion and inquiry; if those quarters that are qualified for the task at last set about giving it a worthy status among modern arts: then my purpose will have been amply fulfilled. I know that in this desire I am at one with a great number of film producers, composers and connoisseurs, who have encouraged me to undertake this book.

In this connection I wish to thank all those who have helped me with their experience and valuable suggestions, and above all Messrs. Arthur Benjamin, Hanns Eisler, Arthur Honegger, Karol Rathaus, Eric Sarnette and Ernest H. Traub. More especially I am indebted to Mr. Paul Rotha for his extremely helpful advice, and to my translator for his unfailing cooperation.

K. L.

London, 1936

Contents

15

Contents

16

Contents

Illustrations

19

Illustrations

Illustrations

Illustrations

Typical example of a film score by Hanns Eisler.
Facsimile of the original MS. from the music for the
film *La nouvelle terre*   *facing page* 230

Example of the music for the Italian film *O la borsa,
o la vita,* composed by Vittorio Rieti
                              facing page 244

Part One: Origins of Film Music

Part One: Origins of Film Music

Show-booth and primitive sound-film

The beginnings of film music, like the earliest attempts at the film itself, are to be found in the dingy interior of the showman's booth. The predecessor of the moving picture was not so much the motionless image, projected from the magic lantern, as the screens of those public showmen at some Continental fairs, who recited blood-curdling ballads in a characteristic singsong while pointing out with a stick the successive illustrations of the main phases of the plot. These pictures were either shown side by side on a large wooden screen, or were displayed singly one after the other. The narrator, whom we find again in later times in front of the canvas screen of the films, did not speak in ordinary tones, but sang. Thus he produced the earliest form of film music. Perhaps such performances will be remembered by some readers who visited the markets in smaller Continental towns round the turn of the century. In a scene of the modern version of *The Beg-*

25

gar's *Opera* (*Dreigroschenoper*), by Kurt Weill, the composer very neatly hits off the characteristic tone of this musical recitative.

The film succeeded the ballad singers and took their place. Its earliest plots were derived, logically enough, from the field of melodrama, which had for centuries maintained itself in popular favour. The interpreters of these shocking stories felt, very rightly, that normal speech did not suffice to infect the imagination of the audience with the desired atmosphere of suspense. So they departed from the idiom of everyday, and raised their voices in declamatory pathos until they reached the pitch of song. They made, sometimes with instrumental accompaniment, music. The pictures thereby gained in vividness in the mind's eye of the onlooker; their inferior and unnatural colours took on a semblance of reality. The characters depicted in them assumed real dimensions and stepped out of their tableaux. The musical accompaniment had created an atmosphere of individuality. The more musically impressive the narrator managed to render his story, the bigger were the audiences he attracted.

This type of performance lost its public as soon as Edison, Lumière and Messter had invented and developed the cinematograph. Most of those who had formerly flocked to the ballad recitals now went to the cinema, which at first hardly differed in its gen-

26

eral features from their old haunts. The first 'films' were shown in a kind of show-booth or similar obscure premises. They were turned at great speed and each lasted only a few minutes. In the beginning, they had as yet no explanatory subtitles, and would, without a commentary, have remained in many cases unintelligible to their simple-minded audience. As a result the narrator was reinstated, to keep the spectators in a good humour and to act as 'compère' to the films, in the tradition of his predecessor, the ballad singer.

Let us try to picture to ourselves the cinema of those days—some out-of-the-way hall, probably rectangular in shape, with a screen in front, the projection machine at the back, and chairs in the intermediate space. The projector made a terrible noise: the commentator had to have good lungs to make his discourse audible. And, between them, we can imagine the young couples rejoicing in the darkness of the place—the biggest attraction of the cinema in those days! In places such as this film music was born.

It began, not as a result of any artistic urge, but from the dire need of something which would drown the noise made by the projector. For in those times there were as yet no sound-absorbent walls between the projection machine and the auditorium. This painful noise disturbed visual enjoyment to no small

extent. Instinctively cinema proprietors had recourse
to music, and it was the right way, using an agreeable sound to neutralise one less agreeable. The first
instruments to be used for the purpose were mechanical: barrel-organ, musical box, orchestrion and—
phonograph.

We reach a period which saw the forerunner of
the sound-film. To put it more accurately, we should
say that the beginnings of the film were at the same
time the beginnings of the sound-film. Just about the
same time as the invention of the living picture,
Edison evolved his phonograph and—a little later—
Berliner the gramophone. On the 6th October 1889
the first 'sound-film' by Edison was performed. The
machine used to exhibit it was called the 'cineto-
phonograph' and was displayed in 1893 at the Chi-
cago World Exposition. A collaborator of Edison's
was seen raising his hat and speaking the classic
words: 'Good morning, Mr. Edison! How do you like
the cinematograph?'

It must, however, be added that this 'sound-film'
could be viewed only by one person at a time, as projection on to the canvas screen was not yet known.
And the duration of the film was necessarily limited
by the small dimensions of the cylinder in the phonograph. But only a few years later Charles Pathé introduced the Berliner gramophone, with its records
running for much longer periods, and invented, to-

gether with his mechanic Joly, a system which made possible a quasi-synchronized performance of the film strip and the gramophone record. In the same year, 1896, Oscar Messter made the same experiment. Quite independently, Paris and Berlin proceeded in the same direction, to a preliminary stage of the later sound-on-disc film.

Of synchronism, in the *modern* sense of the word, there was as yet no trace. Besides, such performances suffered from a perceptible lack of volume, a fault which could not even be eliminated by Messter's attempt to run several gramophones with giant horns simultaneously. There were still no amplifiers: indeed, electro-acoustic science was altogether undeveloped at that time. It was the World War, with its scientific needs, which first brought about a change in this respect.

And so the original sound-film died after only a brief spell of life. Almost a whole generation was still to pass before its triumphant resurrection. The silent film entered on its provisional reign. But, as far as its music was concerned, at the outset the silent film also showed a strong tendency to mechanism; orchestrions and similar instruments, which had the additional advantage of greater resonance, dominated largely. It was only when the film itself began to advance along the road of its artistic development that film music too emerged from its humble origin,

29

and we can well say that from then on the reciprocal effects on each other between film and music stood in equal relation to one another. As the artistic maturity of the film increased, so the individual art of film music assumed at each stage more and more its own definite character. The first period of its development lasted about fifteen years, starting from 1898.

Part Two: Music with the Silent Film

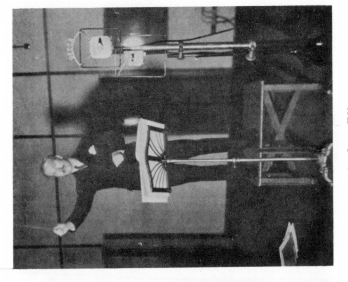

Arthur Bliss

William Walton
Howard Coster Photograph

Arthur Benjamin

Walter Leigh

Part Two: Music with the Silent Film

A. Aesthetics and psychology

If we want to understand the practical uses of music in connection with the silent film, we must first of all shed some light on the aesthetic and psychological background out of which that music developed after the end of the first phase in the history of the film. Let us imagine ourselves back in the days of the silent films. We are sitting in a hall where a film is being shown, and in front of us on the screen the film is rolled off without any musical accompaniment. We are watching a succession of images which are on a plane, that is, have no definite plastic character, and we follow the course of all sorts of destinies and occurrences, without hearing any other sound than the low hum from the projection room. We see people speaking, and no sound is heard; subtitles appear as commentary and substitute for dialogue; life is enacted in a world of almost ghostly silence. The pictures, moreover, are in black and white; for in those days colour films, both in number and quality, played an even more insignificant part than they did, until very recent times, in the world of talking films.

To sum up, films, shown without a sound, on a plane, in a monotonous black and white, were in a manner of speaking dimensionless. The visual element alone and unsupported can never be sufficient substitute for an actual representation of life, and the film, to attain full artistic expression, must make use of more realistic media. So the need of sound or music was still felt, even when the primitive conditions of the early cinema had no longer to be reckoned with.

It must not be thought that music (leaving aside the considerations which prompted its use in the original cinema, which by now were no longer valid) was meant to serve as a compensation for the natural sounds which were absent. A bad impression was made by the attempts of some illustrators of silent films to have their orchestra imitate noises, the original reproduction of which the silent film did not allow. These attempts showed very clearly that the realism of the pictures should on no account reappear in the music, and furthermore that the plastic character of sound (even where synchronism was attained) did not harmonize with the plane dimensions of the picture. Music had a profound effect on this dimensionless character of the film image, the nebulous existence of which was further intensified by the lack of

its own proper sounds. It also enriched the colour-
scheme of the picture in black and white by its variety
of harmonic and instrumental high-lights.

But all these reasons do not suffice to justify its
uses. The need of music with the silent film cannot
simply be explained, from the point of view of mass
psychology, by the discovery that a crowd would
listen in silence, but would not *watch* in silence, without hearing anything as accompaniment. The reason
which is aesthetically and psychologically most essential to explain the need of music as an accompaniment of the silent film, is without doubt *the rhythm
of the film as an art of movement.* We are not accustomed to apprehend movement as an artistic form
without accompanying sounds, or at least audible
rhythms. Every film that deserves the name must
possess its individual rhythm which determines its
form. (Form is here taken in the widest sense as a
ruling concept.) It was the task of the musical accompaniment to give it auditory accentuation and profundity.

Next to rhythm, expression is one of the most important elements of silent-film music, because, owing
to the intrinsic nature of the soundless picture, gesture and mimicry have to act as substitutes for the
spoken word. But these alone would not be enough,
for the power and impression exercised by the spoken
word have a tremendous and decisive effect. Speech

is the foundation of the whole of civilization; and only when a very refined state of culture has been reached can another medium of expression in certain cases be allowed to take its place. In the case of the film, music was this medium, and remained such, to a certain degree, even when the sound-film superseded the silent, because it most happily completes the picture.

Musical accompaniment was needed for the silent film, to bring out that intangible element which had, in the absence of speech and the noises of everyday life, to work on mind and soul through a combination of ear and eye. This does not mean only descriptive music, which by its colouring and programme character 'makes poetry in sound', but also the opposite method, the development of a musical thought derived from the basic idea underlying the film it accompanies, unconcerned with single details or extraneous matter, seemingly running alongside the shots and avoiding all descriptive features, but in reality supporting the film in rhythm, in thought, and in structure. (These two tendencies, the impressionistic and the expressionistic, have always run side by side, often as a matter of fact within one single film.)

Thus we can without risk of exaggeration maintain that it was music, first and alone, which gave the silent film its life-blood, its soul, and its meaning.

36

It laid bare its innermost fibres, and at the same time could throw a veil of impenetrability over it; it dictated the rhythm and bridged over dramaturgical weaknesses; it lent it form and depth, and enlivened its colours; it raised it from the level of a characterless mechanism. The silent film without music had no right to exist.

But then how did one hear film music? Did one hear it at all?

Music heard in the concert-hall differs fundamentally from music heard with films, because absolute music is apprehended *consciously*, film music *unconsciously*. In the course of the musical illustration of a film familiar or characteristic bars of music may have struck the filmgoer once or twice, but otherwise he could hardly have told you, especially in an instance of well-made film music, what he had really heard. Only at points where the music diverged from the picture, whether in its quality or meaning, was his concentration on the picture disturbed. Thus we reach the conclusion that good film music remained 'unnoticed'.

Yet the assumption that music accompanying a silent film did not have great importance would be very wide of the mark. It is true to say that film music was heard with the greatest intensity, because everything that is apprehended by the subconscious

37

self is much more deeply impressed on a man than conscious experience. For the same consciousness which fulfils the functions of everyday life requires from the average man a slow process of working things out, and of the gradual storage of them in his brain, by means of deduction. The combined effect of visual and auditory impressions in the cinema, however, enhances the speed of intuitive perception, facilitates it by concrete means and guides it into the subconscious mind; and, although the percepts are not thereby at once fixed in the human brain, yet they are introduced by indirect paths into the general mental organism, which will then naturally find it much easier to analyse them later in conscious thought.

So the purpose and character of a piece of film music was brought home, even to the least musical of laymen, sooner and with greater effect than would have been possible in the case of a symphony, or even an operatic score. That was a tremendous advantage, and is so even to-day in sound-films, at every point where music is used to interpret the film strip for the purpose of dramatic completeness, as for instance when speech and other sounds cease. An unconscious education in music itself, of a public that once had been without interest in music, was accomplished as the orchestra came more and more to be used in the silent-film theatre; the awakening of an active interest in music amongst a great part of the cinema public imposed a considerable responsibility upon film composers, a responsibility which the sound-film in no way lessened, but actually, owing to the greater variety of its artistic form, increased.

B. From pianist to orchestra

With the entry of the pianist as the musical accompanist of the film, the first period of mechanical music in the cinema came to an end. At the outset, his repertoire remained a matter of complete indifference; he played anything he liked, and there was little or no connection between music and the film it accompanied. Only gradually did he begin to make a more exact musical differentiation between one film and another. In this process popular 'song hits' played a considerable part, as their well-known titles produced certain associations of ideas in the minds of the audience. If the player was clever, he played the piano with one hand and the harmonium with the other; and so it very often happened that his right hand knew not what his left hand did. . . .

An improvement both in the quality and quantity of films was first required, before good musicians could be engaged in the service of the cinema. In the beginning of the pianist period there were often incidents, because the audience could not get used to the execution of the 'pianist'. There used to be current an anecdote about a man in a cinema audience who had been sitting in long-suffering silence while a very bad pianist accompanied the film. When the heroine was about to seek an end of her troubles by plunging to a watery grave, he called out to her image on the screen, in a voice full of disgust: 'Take the pianist with you, while you're about it!'

There existed in those days no literature of film music, yet there was a reluctance to turn the treasures of classical and more modern serious music to the uses of the cinema, because the pictures, as a form of entertainment, still ranked low in the social scale. So the better musicians frequently improvised. They abandoned themselves to their moods, as prompted by the pictures, and expressed them in a medley of their own and other people's music, free from any convention of style. They thereby had recourse instinctively to an ideal form of silent-film music: *improvisation*. But this form was destined to remain a solecism, and it naturally fell into disuse as the average cinema grew larger.

And now the film itself started on its very swift ascent. Out of the short moving picture was developed the film strip that was miles long, and from the initial enthusiasm for ridiculously exaggerated movement there arose, gradually enough, a disciplined rhythm in the photography. Quantity grew with quality. Film-writing became more ambitious as the potentialities of the camera were increased; plots became more and more complicated; directors were less and less restricted by technical limitations; while the actors played in a new simplified style. At the same time more was demanded of the costumes and scenery; at the beginning of the film's career, these could only be matched for primitiveness and lack of taste by the halls in which the films were exhibited. Badly exposed exteriors were superseded by studio productions which were the result of most carefully planned photographic technique; and it was not long before the transparent roofs of the 'glass-houses' lost their *raison d'être*: the film technicians evolved their own better lighting.

It was only natural, as a consequence of this development, that cinemas should also improve. They grew in size, and their decoration was suited to the fastidious tastes of an urban audience. The film advanced farther and farther away from the old show-booth, and finally was ashamed of its dingy origin, which—in the age-old fashion of the parvenu—it attempted to conceal by pomp and splendour. In spite of that, it took a very long time before it managed to win friends in that section of the population which made up the main contingent of the theatre public. We can safely assert that the Great War first made the decisive breach: before the complete revolution in all values which the War brought in its train, the film, despite all its efforts, still remained an outsider.

As the requirements of the cinema grew more elaborate, so more was expected of the music it offered. And this was a matter dictated, not only by considerations of film music but also by a desire to attract the public, the best part of whom was heartily sick of the experiments with pianists. Out of the nucleus consisting of piano and harmonium a small enlargement of forces was at first made with strings (violins and violoncelli); then there came the chamber orchestra in its various combinations, and finally, in the last few years of the silent-film period, the big cinema palaces were served by orchestras which, composed as they were of 50 to 100 musicians, put to shame many a medium-sized city orchestra.

Parallel with this development a new career for conductors offered itself: they had to lead the cinema orchestra and select the illustrative music. Prominent men often filled these posts with salaries which more often than not exceeded that of an opera conductor. And at the same time a flourishing occupation was that of compiling music for the purpose of illustrating silent films; in rare cases there were actually original compositions.

That the orchestra, once available, supplemented the preliminary programme with musical entertainment, followed as a matter of course. The ambition of some conductors led them on such occasions to tackle major works of the classical and romantic periods. Thus the audience in the first-night houses of the silent-film period enjoyed the advantage of buying concert tickets simultaneously with their entrance tickets, and millions of visitors to cinemas suddenly consumed a huge and unprecedented amount of music. Live music (wireless and gramophone transmissions had, moreover, recently become things of everyday life) witnessed an enormous boom, whereas it would otherwise have been limited to the comparatively small circle of opera and concert audiences.

In this way, as a natural result, a multitude of problems presented themselves. A hesitant beginning was made with the analysis of aesthetic aspects of film music. Attempts were made to establish the forms of illustrative combinations, or compilations, as they were called, and of original film compositions. The structure of the film itself was all the time being more and more carefully planned, and this meant a corresponding tendency to pay more attention to the musical part of the performance as well. On the other hand, the musicians' lot was not made any easier by strange methods of organizing production and distribution. Faulty arrangements and the opposition between individual firms and cinemas led to a position in which the conductor had in most cases one or two days, and in the big first-night houses a little longer in rare instances, at his disposal for the musical treatment of the film. It often happened that the compilation was completed the night before, the rehearsal took place the following morning, and in the afternoon the first performance was already due. The composer, likewise, had to work all the time with an anxious eye upon the calendar: he had exceptional luck if he ever could obtain four weeks' grace for music that was to last one and a half hours in performance, and had to thank the producing firm and the director for such special favour. For they regarded music for films at best as a necessary evil.

There were thus a number of obstacles in face of the free development of film music, due not least to the indifference of the daily press to this aspect of the cinema. The evolution took place in the second fifteen-year period of the silent film, between 1913 and 1928, the year, to all intents and purposes, when the sound-film made its *début*. But, whereas the preceding period only witnessed a technical and not an artistic advance, the succeeding stage already brought all the seeds of the future with it. For this reason a closer examination of the musical accompaniment of the silent film is essential to the understanding of what came later.

C. The silent-film orchestra

The composition of the silent-film orchestra was subject in general to the same rules and conditions in every case, if we take as our example the larger picture-theatres, in which alone a kind of musical culture could flourish at all. These used flutes, clarinets, trumpets, trombones, percussion and pianoforte. Usually there was an organ (built into the big houses) or harmonium to compensate for the missing wind-instruments and to give greater effect to dynamic variations. Only in rare cases were horns employed. Of course, the strings, in the shape of a few violins, violoncelli and a double-bass, were not dispensed with; but only quite a few cinema orchestras could afford the luxury of viola parts. The advantage of an orchestra so composed, capable of having its numbers strengthened, in the strings especially, lay not alone in the saving in individual players, but also in the fact that it had at its disposal a huge literature without extra arrangement of the parts: for either it could easily be adapted, or it was available in the

46

parts that made up the so-called chamber orchestra. This literature included the whole of light music and also, in arranged form, portions of favourite works by famous masters, the use of which became more and more frequent. For the needs of film music, this form of orchestra was fully adequate. The peculiar qualities of film music in those early days already permitted a much slighter orchestral scheme, and could dispense with a huge symphonic body of players who might possibly kill the picture with their mass of sound, because the spectator's attention would be distracted from the screen. As soon as there was a case of failure to keep the right proportion between the dynamic properties of the film and its accompaniment, a conflict was bound to take place between the two for the attention of the audience. So the manning of the orchestra was not the decisive factor as regards the quality of film music.

The 'piano lead', a pianoforte text reproducing in outline all the important instrumental parts, was substituted for the full score. If one or another instrument was missing, it certainly involved a change in the sound-colouring, but the melodic line was transferred to other parts, and thus preserved. This practice often meant a considerable sacrifice of effect, when significant solo parts were remodelled, quite against the meaning of the music, or even had to fall away altogether. In any event, it was hard to secure the balance of sound between wind and strings, which seldom stood in the right proportion. In general, the parts were: 4 first and 2 second violins, 1 or 2 'celli and 1 double-bass, against 3 or 4 wood-wind and as many brass, with piano and percussion, to which an organ or harmonium had to be added.

Even in these problems, which are concerned solely with orchestral technique, we can see that traditional conceptions of the symphony orchestra and the employment of its established components were altogether inappropriate. (The introduction of jazz instruments must be noted here, but they were used with surprising reserve.) The cinema conductor, if he was at all a conscientious musician, had, before he even ascended his desk, to tackle a host of problems to which the operatic conductor is a complete stranger. Whilst every effort to perform clearly orchestrated music was to be made, under no circumstances was it to be tolerated that the mere outline of a piece of music be heard, and not its final form, which was essential to the illustration of the film.

After he had settled the instrumental questions, the creative work of the leader of the orchestra began. Here, too, we mean the musical directors of the principal theatres: for the conductors of the smaller cinemas generally followed their lead, as they received the musical arrangements, the work of

Edmund Meisel (standing in front of the orchestra)
shortly before his death, during the rehearsals for
the Russian silent film *The Blue Express. Unpub-
lished private photograph, taken by his wife*

Synchronisation-room for the Topoly system

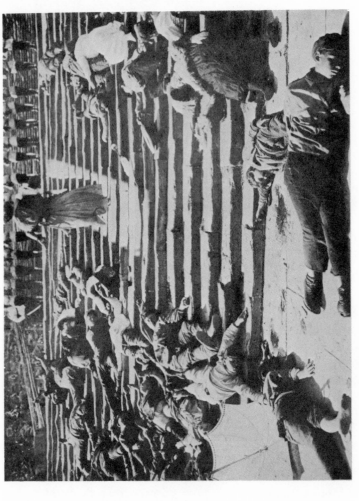

Battleship Potemkin by S. M. Eisenstein. (The famous scene on the steps of Odessa.) Edmund Meisel's music for that film made film music history

their more prominent colleagues, together with the roll of film containing the picture. They could alter the score according to their own individual needs or taste.

D. Illustration; compiled music (Kinothek)

Two kinds of music accompanied the silent film: music made up of already existing pieces strung together (compiled), ordinarily called illustration; and original compositions. Let us first look at the practice of illustration.

In its primitive form, this had already been introduced by the more skilful exponents of pianoforte accompaniment. Well-known pieces, the character of which was considered by the pianist to correspond best with the individual scenes in the film, were selected and played one after the other, partly without artistic connection, that is, without modulation or transition of any sort, and partly joined into one whole by improvised modulations. This practice was taken over by the orchestras, and was by them elaborated with skilful, specially composed transitions between the various pieces. They began to base their choice of music on more profound ideas of psychology and characterisation. For this purpose, there rapidly

50

came into general use a unique kind of music, namely that which the Italian Giuseppe Becce first published in Berlin under the name of *Kinothek* (a contraction of *Kinobibliothek,* or cinema library). It soon found imitators all over the world, so that finally a library of

Typical example of a piece from Becce's *Kinothek.* This piece belongs to the very first printed *Kinothek.* (Reproduction of the first print, 1919.)

several thousands of small single pieces in all conceivable moods and characters was built up.

51

'Illustration'—how is the word to be understood in the film-musical sense? Illustrative or descriptive music, so-called programme music, is no modern invention. It dates from the infancy of music. But whereas absolute programme music pursues a programme of the composer's choice, and builds it up within a musical form, in film-musical illustration we have an accompaniment adapted to the sense of the events visible on the screen. The music cannot therefore develop any given process of thought logically according to its own forms, but must conform to the scenario, which is rolled off on the film without any consideration for the logical thought and form of the music. Music is no longer the mistress, but the servant, in the process. For this reason alone the conjunction of alien and stylistically opposed types of music could be recognised: for it was no longer a question of autonomous form. So, although at that time the artistic value of the compilation process was greatly overestimated, it would, on the other hand, be a serious mistake to give way to indignation because music by great composers was torn out of the original contexts and coupled with music of lesser worth by other hands. For, however desirable it was that the film should be supplied with music specially composed for it, this could hardly be done with all the hundreds of films used in the space of a single year by the big countries; such special treatment had to be reserved for a small group of the biggest and most expensive pictures (which were not necessarily always the best).

A good illustration involved much more than a mere juxtaposition of single pieces: any musician could have managed that, if he commanded the technique and the literature. The essential thing was a kind of metamorphosis, a transformation of the given material into a single whole, which had to conform to the rhythm, the meaning, and the colouring of the film. In conjunction with a film, a good illustration had without doubt certain artistic values which could, if specially effective, be turned to commercial uses.

Illustration in the shape of compiled music is, we may observe, by no means a new thing. Its predecessor was the old 'Selection'. It is also a well-known fact that as far back as two hundred years ago operatic arias were smuggled into church music, and church cantatas interpolated into operas. In the same way, compilations are found wherever light music is played in potpourri form. Such a past is not calculated to make a very good impression, and so the reserve of serious musicians can readily be understood.

If at that time illustration was greatly overestimated, there is no reason to reject it completely. The compiler had to weld together his material on the basis of the film, and bring order into chaos. In this sense, he could to a certain degree be rated equally with an original composer. Even pieces which were characteristic in themselves could have their nature transformed in the melting-pot of compilation. There arose a new style, which absorbed all the earlier individuality of the single pieces in favour of a new collective character. This went so far that even the rhythm, tempo, key, form, instrumentation, and actually the melody of a piece of music had to be remodelled.

This arbitrary treatment made the use of renowned works of great masters, which appeared in increasingly large quantities in the repertoires of film musicians, a knotty problem indeed. On the one hand, serious music was indispensable; on the other hand, often enough it was not allowed to retain its own character. Change in its form was the least significant thing which could happen to it. As a result, more and more use was made of the *Kinothek*, originated by Giuseppe Becce in the year 1919.

Here we have, for the first time in the history of modern music, a systematic tabulation of music according to its uses. Without the slightest regard for sentiment, the illustrator had a catalogued library made for him, collected from a host of small pieces of music which could be played through in not more than a few minutes each. This library grew with the momentum of an avalanche as the films won their emancipation. It contained, if we follow the romantic conception of programme music, all the moods of men and the elements, every kind of reaction to human destiny, musical drawings of nature and animals, of peoples and countries: in short, every sphere of life, well and clearly arranged under headings. Within this cinematographic library there were of course also arrangements of characteristic pieces by well-known composers of every rank.

The commonest heads under which the catalogue was drawn up can be found in the *Handbook of Film Music* by Erdmann, Becce and Brav. Here there is a plan of a universally valid subdivision into certain main concepts, which are again analysed under subordinate headings. Appended below are a few examples of this pigeon-holing:

DRAMATIC EXPRESSION (Main concept)
1. CLIMAX (Subordinate concept)
   (*a*) Catastrophe; (Subdivisions)
   (*b*) Highly dramatic *agitato*;
   (*c*) Solemn atmosphere; mysteriousness of nature.

2. TENSION—*Misterioso*
   (*a*) Night: sinister mood;
   (*b*) Night: threatening mood;
   (*c*) Uncanny *agitato*;

(*d*) Magic: apparition;

(*e*) Impending doom: 'something is going to happen.'

3. TENSION—*Agitato*

(*a*) Pursuit, flight, hurry;

(*b*) Fight;

(*c*) Heroic combat;

(*d*) Battle;

(*e*) Disturbance, unrest, terror;

(*f*) Disturbed masses: tumult;

(*g*) Disturbed nature: storm, fire.

4. CLIMAX—*Appassionato*

(*a*) Despair;

(*b*) Passionate lament;

(*c*) Passionate excitement;

(*d*) Jubilant;

(*e*) Victorious;

(*f*) Bacchantic.

Other main concepts were: dramatic scenes; lyrical expression; lyrical incident; quite general incident, subdivided again into three subordinate headings, Nature (romantically descriptive), Nation and Society, Church and State. The possible variations in the subheadings were of course exceedingly numerous and set no bounds to the compiler's imagination.

It was no wonder that a catalogue made on such schematic lines could easily become stereotyped;

this disadvantage from the artistic point of view was more than compensated by its quicker and ever more effective application.

The musical form of these *Kinotheks* was very elementary. Since it had to be recognised that their use was confined to short episodes, the music had to be quite simple in form, so that a division into its musical components could be made without loss of its original characteristics. So even the simplest of musical forms, the song form, could not always be recommended, because, in the tripartite scheme A—B—A, the middle part differs in character from the first and last parts. The most useful form was a continuous piece lasting about two or three minutes, of a uniform character, where possible with a single theme running through it, with the same descriptive categories as its basis, and of homogeneous tonality and structure.

Within these limits it naturally depended on the talent of the composer whether he could create something above the merely useful. Variations of the theme, for instance, inversions, inconspicuous changes of key, alterations of tempo without affecting the rhythmical character of the music, all offer an opportunity for individual and charming features. Becce's *Kinotheks* are a veritable mine of all the typical characteristics of this kind of music.

Already existing passages of music had to be prepared for inclusion in the *Kinothek* on corresponding lines. Their technical value for the film illustrator was increased, according as they could be used in effecting a quick compilation. If the illustrator had first had to work out the appropriate bars selected, let us say, from the score of a symphony, he would never have finished within the prescribed period.

The illustrator's work proceeded roughly as follows. He first carefully looked at the film, in order to gain an impression of its content and form. Then at a second performance of the film, in sections, he calculated accurately, with a stop-watch, the times taken in playing the single scenes which he intended to divide musically one from another. After that, the selection of the music began. At this stage, it depended on whether the illustration was to be a compilation of numbers, exactly in the style of the old opera, or, more like the music drama, a psychological arrangement in *Leitmotiv—Leitmotiv*, not in the strict sense of the term, as it appears in Wagner's scores: that would have been impossible, because the film, unlike the music drama with its slow development, advances by leaps and bounds, and, owing to the short duration of its individual scenes, would not allow the themes any clear growth. *Leitmotiv* in film music cannot be anything else than the title for a predominant mood, a characteristic sentiment, or the delineation of a person, which may assist the spec-

58

tator's understanding, and perhaps also shed some psychological light on the film. It must never, as in Wagner, become a fundamental structural principle. So it happened that in general the prevailing form was that of numbers, with occasional quotations of a few main themes in a style approaching the *Leitmotiv*.

In the number form, the most essential numbers are at the same time the climaxes of the film. (This is exactly the sense in which modern opponents of the music drama and defenders of the musical theatre expound the use of themes in their dramaturgy.) This substructure was finished off with a quantity of other pieces or sections of pieces. Very often single sections were simply set side by side and played without any transition, sometimes only with a short modulation, when the contrast of styles seemed too crude. At the same time, in a more developed stage of illustration, there were modulations constructed on quite a big scale, and even the illustrator's own specially composed interludes. Often enough these short passages had the greatest value, because they were created out of the feeling originally inspired by the film itself, and were at once transformed into music, whereas the compilations were at best only substitutes.

The silent film did not require a close interpretation of *all* its separate scenes; what it required was the opposite, the *musical simplification of the mosaic*

of film images into one long line. The even flow of
the music must therefore, apart from certain exceptions based on dramatic considerations, not be inter-
rupted. The chief idea was usually to find a recon-
ciliation between the various pieces, and that was
not always easy, even when two successive numbers
were very similar in style. It is possible, by means of
rhythmic and melodic modulations, to produce a
connection between two pieces, no matter how different in character. But the swift turning of the film
strip and the quick changes in scene made this practically impossible: *one* such modulation in the traditional sense of the term, and the film would have
rushed several yards past the music. So the problem
was to find some method of avoiding too quick and
jerky changes in the music, without destroying the
significant line of the film. Variety in the film
images and uniformity in the music: this was the required combination.

The personal taste of the illustrator set its stamp
on the selection of his pieces. There were cinema
conductors who avoided compilations and accompanied good films with fragments out of the works of
one single composer. This happened at times with
music by Debussy and Tschaikowsky. In such cases
it was possible to avoid interrupting the line of the
music too often and mixing up the styles, for even
when the music changed the style could be preserved

60

in all its essential features. But mostly musicians found themselves forced to make use of the *Kinothek,* if only because of the great number of mediocre films which came out in rapid succession. So it was mainly a question of skill in making as good and ingenious transitions as possible. This method was the simplest, and the man who mastered it and easily recognised the transitional bars could dispense with modulations and speed up his work. The more appropriate and skilful the compilations, the easier became the technique of transition.

If, however, modulations were unavoidable, they had to have quite a different appearance from those in symphonic music, for instance. For while in the latter transitions are founded on the flow and the form of the music, and so are once for all part and parcel of art, the film musician's idea of modulation is, oddly enough, reduced once more to its original starting-point of pure expediency. In the case of the film-musical modulation, all that matters is to obtain connections between sections of music that differ in character, as well and as quickly as possible. In a film we have no time for reflection. The film strip rushes irresistibly on. So it did not matter whether the principles of musical modulation were observed a little more or less in the compilation. It mattered above all things that the transitions should disturb neither the rhythm nor the character of the music.

E. Original composition

The system of compiled film illustrations remained, even in its greatest perfection, only a makeshift. Original composition had to be the artistic goal, even in the period of the silent film. That so few silent films were furnished with music specially composed, was not only due to a lack of understanding in production; there were many technical difficulties in performance which had to be overcome before success was possible. The 'general release' theatres did not possess completely equipped orchestras. It could not be expected of music publishers that they should print this kind of music, save for a few self-contained numbers which they brought out for concert and light entertainment purposes. It would have been much too costly and unprofitable to publish, as it would have involved the printing of several arrangements for different orchestral combinations. The film companies would not entertain the idea of taking shares in, or themselves taking charge of, the publishing; for them, original music

62

was, if not a mere luxury, at best a good means of propaganda, intended to heighten the general impression among press and other interested parties at the first performance of the film. They did not think of the general public which would see the same film with inadequate music and go away with an inadequate impression. This music, too, was often boycotted by ambitious conductors in the local houses, because they wished to compile their own, and because a quick and good rehearsal was for technical reasons impossible.

The constant difficulties, when the film company had once decided to incur the expense of original music, were almost invariably due to the fearful haste in which the musicians had to work. The film was finished, the theatre for the first performance chosen. That occasion, with luck, might be three to four weeks distant from the start of the composer's work; it must see the score ready for performance. The quantity of the music corresponded roughly to that contained in a small opera. . . .

The composer at the outset went about his task in the same way as the illustrator, in most cases. He became acquainted with the film, and then measured his individual scenes with a stop-watch, an average speed of sixteen film frames per second, in contrast to the twenty-four used in connection with sound-films, being the standard of reckoning. During

63

the performance he remained in constant communication with the operator, because in certain places the speed would be increased, in others diminished.

The composer could also show himself the film on his own, on a table fitted up for the purpose. As soon as all the sections were accurately labelled with their time-measurement in minutes and seconds, the composition could begin.

Like the illustrator, the experienced composer made dramatic climaxes his starting-points and, out of the musical foundations built on this basis, developed the form and structure of the other sections. As he himself created the music according to the nature of the film and could conceive it in the spirit of the film's plot, he naturally commanded opportunities quite different from those of the illustrator, who had to stick to finished pieces. Most film musicians composed only after the scene to be put into music had been divided into strokes marking the beat, wherein meticulous accuracy was vouchsafed by metronome and stop-watch. There were also a very few experts who could determine the required length of music with a somnambulist's certainty, without using any other ordinary resource available for the purpose. These had all the greater latitude in their work.

The composer of a film had to keep watch, not only on the exact correspondence in length between pic-

Carl Robert Blum at his rhythmonome, reading off
a tape with the note-signs

Rhythmoscope. An apparatus to secure the synchronism of the rhythm-tape with the rhythm

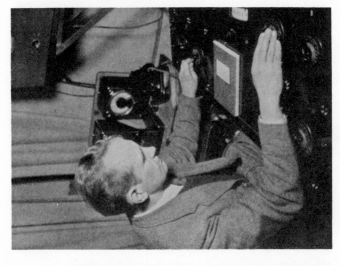

Recording Director at the sound-control table

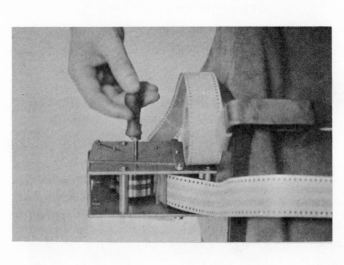

Marking-line machine for the notes on the rhythm-tape

ture and music but also on the concentration of the musical form. As we have seen, there had been in the traditional theory of forms neither norm nor precedent for this, unless the old form of composition in a 'theme with variations' were transferred to the needs of the film.

The film composer had already at that time a difficult position. He had to be servant and master at one and the same time. He had to subordinate himself to the work, and avoid any too pretentious personal styles, without in any way abandoning the characteristic profile of his writing. He had to consider the necessarily simple structure of film music, and strike the true balance between homophonic and polyphonic composition. It was his duty to respect the needs of the smaller theatres and make allowance for the fact that any really difficult technique in his score could seldom be overcome by cinema orchestras.

F. Attempts at synchronisation

The performance of this music, wherein the correspondence with the picture had in the nature of things to be even more exact than in interchangeable compilations, was a problem which musicians and technicians worked hard to master in the later years of the silent film. Various inventions cropped up which had as their object the greatest possible synchronism between film strip and music. In Berlin Carl Robert Blum erected his music chronometer, out of which the later system of rhythmography (more recently termed phonorhythmy) for the doubling of sound-films was developed.

This instrument, subsequently called the *rhythmonome*, Blum had been evolving since 1919, and he exhibited it in public for the first time in 1926 in Berlin. It is intended to 'register the living rhythm of music, speech, or other successions of sounds "phonorhythmically" by electrical recording on a tape running at a determinable speed. In this way the time-values of such sounds are translated

66

into corresponding space-values. Every rhythm in sound is thereby rendered apparent to sight. This "rhythmogram" is thus the optical representation of otherwise rhythmical sound-processes, as the phonogram is their acoustical reproduction.'

This is Blum's own definition of the rhythmonome's function, and this explanation already anticipates its mode of application to the sound-film.

The rhythmonome works as follows. Tapes registering the 'phonorhythmical' signs run within the instrument in such a way that they pass a sight-index from left to right, that is, in the direction of reading. The sound can then be reproduced in the original rhythm, as the sight-index allows it to be read off in exact timing. The rhythmonome can thus be contrasted with the metronome, for, whereas the latter gives the metrical distribution (in equal beats), the former presents the ametrical (irregular) pulsations, that is, *the living rhythm*. We shall have cause to return to these illuminating principles evolved by Blum, when we deal with the synchronisation of sound-films.

So the rhythmo-tapes, even in the rhythmonome of the silent-film period, registered the successive stages in the main current of the music. The instrument was placed on the conductor's desk and was coupled in synchronism with the film projector; the running speed could be constantly controlled by

67

means of a 'musical chronometer'. The conductor only had to guide his orchestra in such a way that the music was timed to sound at every point exactly as the corresponding notes ran past the sight-index.

This very practical instrument could be used to great effect, not only in connection with film music but also in the performance of ordinary music, as for instance was the case at the *première* of Křenek's opera *Johnny spielt auf* at Leipzig in 1927.

In Paris, at about the same time, Pierre de la Commune invented the *cinépupitre*, which Honegger used for the first time for his musical accompaniment to the Abel Gance film *La Roue* (1922). The principles underlying this instrument are very like those of the rhythmonome, but they were not so consistently developed and worked out as Blum's ideas.

Among other attempts to solve the problem of synchronism between silent film and living music, a few more systems which were less successful may be mentioned: for instance, a picture of a conductor was shown on the screen in front of the actual conductor, who, however, could only manage to follow the other's baton with moderate success. Or a ribbon showing the notes of the music was photographed on the lower edge of the film image, and, as with the rhythmonome, registered the synchronization in the middle of the picture; but this disturbed the spectators considerably. A few other inventions could be mentioned only as curiosities, and we can therefore omit them here.

Generally the conductor contented himself with an extremely vague synchronisation. For a man who was inexperienced in film work, the conducting of a cinema orchestra was accordingly almost impossible: a notable instance occurred on the occasion of the first performance of the film of the *Rosenkavalier* in the Dresden State Opera House, when the composer, Richard Strauss, after several vain attempts to keep the orchestra in time with the picture, had to give up his baton in favour of an expert cinema conductor. This is a significant pointer to the position at the time, as in other respects technical problems would not cause any difficulty at all to a specialist like Strauss.

In view of this lack of absolute synchronism, failure attended successive attempts to produce out-and-out musical films: even such aids as the rhythmonome gave only a relative synchronism to the silent film and its accompaniment, the results, from a mechanical point of view, being far from perfect. A film opera was one of the experimental productions of the time. A strip of music printed on to the lower rim of the film image gave the conductor and the singers in the orchestra pit their cues. But the plane dimensions of the picture on the one hand, and the

69

plastic character of the ringing music on the other, did not coincide. Even with a relatively exact synchronism, this experiment would have been doomed to failure. It was contrary to the inherent character of the silent film, not only from a musical point of view but also as regards the peculiar dramatic structure of the silent picture, with its short scenes and its cutting, which were necessarily timed at considerable speed. Very rarely could a scene be enacted longer than usual. This is, by the way, a fundamental difference between the silent and the sound-film.

As long as the film remained silent, there was only one method of musical accompaniment for it: the comprehensive line that was compiled or composed, and not built up on absolute synchronism.

G. Form, rhythm, line, colour

This connection between the dramatic line and the flow of the music (on account of the faulty construction of many films, very often an almost insoluble problem for the musician) raised various questions in regard to the formal construction of the music. These could, it must be remembered, only be solved in connection with the pictures, because traditional musical forms, as we have already seen, with the sole exception of the 'theme with variations', did not lend themselves to film music.

Even if a silent film was, by way of exception, 'symphonically' built, it could not be accompanied in musically symphonic form, but had to be musically focussed and developed from its climaxes. It follows from this that the literary form of a drama, the construction of which is somewhat analogous to that of a classical symphony, is similarly unsuitable for the creation of a film. To-day we know very well that the actual dramaturgy of the film has given the decisive impetus to the decay of the drama. Modern

71

drama (which actually is no longer drama, in the traditional sense of the word), with a method of composition that has changed completely, has departed from the old scheme of

Exposition
Introduction of the dramatic conflict
Development
Climax, Dénouement
Conclusion.

The symphony, again, the composition of which is based on a corresponding scheme:

Introduction
Main and subsidiary theme
Development
Recapitulation
Coda,

would no longer be its old self, if it were to abandon this classical form to the extent that the film has departed from the classical drama.

Besides, the very real fact had to be faced that most films (and unfortunately the sound-film has not brought a great change in this respect) were not composed according to any artistically preconceived form at all, and that not only did the rhythm of the film as a whole suffer thereby but it quite simply was non-existent. Faced with the task of illustrating or composing for an unrhythmical film, which consisted of a shapeless juxtaposition and succession of single episodes, even the most skilful of film musicians could only make an attempt to retouch the weakest spots with clever musical passages.

The rhythm of a film is derived from the various elements in its dramatic composition, and on the rhythm again is based the articulation of the style as a whole. A falsely conceived or falsely constructed rhythm, for example one which was in internal or in external contradiction to the action, ruined the style of the silent film, just as it would to-day ruin that of the sound-film. If there was no rhythm at all in the film, the illustrator had it as his plain duty to trace and focus it by his music—to give the film, so to speak, a backbone by means of musical rhythm. In this respect, directors' lack of musical sense and cutters' want of rhythmical sense had much to answer for. Only rarely did it happen that the director of a film got into touch with his musical colleague, either to cut according to the music, or to alter the cut version as the needs of music and rhythm might dictate. The film industry, organized as it is on purely commercial lines, has often made such co-operation fruitless, even in cases where it might have existed, and thereby robbed itself of a potent weapon. The most striking evidence of its possible force was shown, for example, in the film *Potemkin*:

73

the music by Edmund Meisel, at that time the most modern of the silent-film composers, was so exactly adapted in form and movement to Eisenstein's film that the effect of the pictures was heightened, and indeed achieved an overwhelming hold on the audience, unparalleled in the history of the film.

In addition to these fundamental stylistic conceptions of rhythm and form, there are a few other aesthetic problems which, though of lesser significance, yet do fall within the province of film music, inasmuch as they are also general questions which arise in descriptive music as a whole: association of ideas, folklore, in short, programme music. The term 'programme music' is too well known to need discussion here.

Two theories of descriptive music are important for the film: the explicitly programmatic, or impressionistic, and the interpretative, or expressionistic. The former was more popular with the silent film owing to its greater effect on the audience. The second was preferred by modern musicians, who felt the determining factor for their musical accompaniment to be not so much purely illustrative considerations as the rhythm and the basic psychology of the film. This point of view gained considerable ground later in connection with sound-films.

It would lead us too far from our subject, were we to try to summarise all of those theories (the anti-

nomy has by now become historic) which had to
serve the illustrator as standards for programme
music with the film. Looking back, we can see that
many sins were committed, because the majority of
film musicians were out for mere effect. Musical
quotations from the period are eloquent of this. And
yet the greatest reserve was actually called for, because film music is always bad when it is fussily and
without reason pushed to the front. In addition to
this, the problem of the dramatic connection beween
picture and music involved special difficulties. As we
have already hinted, there very easily arises an inherent discrepancy in a film between the scenes
and the musical accompaniment, because the speed
at which these pictures change is not in keeping
with the character of music, which needs a certain
time to develop. This fact is one of the most essential to the recognition of rhythmical theory in the
film.

The scenes and entrances of the drama are, in the
film, replaced by the cutting; in silent films, this
gave unlimited scope for variations at will within the
individual groups of scenes, so long as these groups
remained as comprehensible units. The uniform
line had to be preserved, and the film prevented
from falling apart into little mosaic fragments.

To take a practical example, let us assume the following passage of a scenario:

1st picture: Sudden spring storm in the mountains;
2nd picture: Mountaineers climbing to the rescue with stretchers;
3rd picture: Crannies in the rocks, sheltering tourists, who are exhausted and cannot go on (long shots and close-ups);
4th picture: Mountain village in the storm;
5th picture: Peasants and their families waiting for news;
6th picture: Others arranging an impromptu service of supplication.

Here we have six scenes which could be characterised by five different musical numbers, assuming that pictures 1 and 4 are musically identical. The single numbers would be very short, some lasting only a few seconds. Instead of this, the illustrator had to accompany the whole group of scenes with a single musical item essentially unvaried in character; and if, for example, the cutter had inserted a picture alien to the context, all that would be necessary to make the transition would be a short interruption in the musical line, for instance a *tremolo* or a chord held on a beat—no piece with a new message, for that would have disturbed the line, and thus the underlying mood, of the whole.

Cinema conductors had at their disposal several adequate, if primitive, means of varying the emphasis, such as change of key, variation in expression, or sharpening of the rhythm. In this connection, rhythm did not only play its fundamental part as the general plan underlying the film, it also developed individual features based on the picture: as, for example, the march of soldiers, dance, or certain gestures and movements. Here film music borrowed from the resources of the dumb show. Again, variation in the speed of projection, which, in contrast to that of the sound-film, used not to remain constant, was a device which could be reserved for especial emphasis.

Part Two: Music with the Silent Film

H. Brief flowering of the cinema orchestra

The evolution of the silent film embraced two almost equal periods of about fifteen years each. In the second of these, which lasted approximately from 1913 to 1928, the silent film became a fine art. Within its defined limits (its two dimensions, the black and white of the images, the restricted area of the screen, and its silence), it achieved a mature form, and produced a few standard works of art that can be said to have left their mark on the history of dramatic art as a whole.

At the same time, the cultivation of music in the cinema theatres reached an astonishingly high level. (Here again this refers to the larger houses: the smaller, with the exception of those managed by artistically inclined proprietors, have never lost their old noisy atmosphere to this day. Yet no one should make the mistake of judging the film by its murkiest examples alone, for even the theatre had, and still

has, its penny gaff.) The presence of the orchestra
led to solo recitals. Musical programmes were more
ambitious and the performances of better quality.
The musicians of the biggest cinemas, with their
well-known and popular conductors, were an inde-
pendent attraction: and the cinema, which had become the staple entertainment of an enormous proportion of the population, began to fulfil a social mis-
sion by turning itself into a purveyor of good music.

It was the great merit of the silent film that it
made the cinema a sanctuary of musicianly playing,
and so performed a task of the highest cultural importance. From the moment when the music of the
cinema exercised its own positive influence, the significance of the film from the social point of view
underwent a fundamental change. With the help of
music, it has become what it is today. A completely
new aspect of musical performance was revealed,
and a completely new idea of ordinary music arose.
Without the film-musical development of the silent
film, a clarification of style would have been impossible, and film makers would have known even less
than they do about their aims.

It was the work of amateurs and quacks, and also
due to the lack of understanding shown by an industry which was purely commercially inclined, and
to the unmusical ears of a number of prominent
film directors, that this development was held up

79

longer than was necessary or, rather, diverted into wrong channels. But the common sense of the public and the eternal truth of artistic principles—they shape themselves, when they have as yet no tradition to support them—would not be denied their ultimate goal.

Then came the sound-film, and with it a strange mechanical interlude. A relapse to the very early stages of primitive cinematography took place. The change-over from the silent to the sound-film brought too great a shock in its train: it was too difficult, both technically and psychologically. This reaction was not only the swing of the pendulum, but also evidence of the difficulty experienced by the human brain in switching over to a new mode of thought. Today, quite a number of years since the first appearance of the sound-film, we have a clearer view of the development which has taken place; and the picture of the film of the future stands before us all the more plainly. We know how much we owe to the silent film and its music. That is why it has seemed necessary to treat the days preceding the sound-film in greater detail than may at first have been thought practical or valuable. Everything in creation has its history, and only when we are acquainted with that, are we in a position to understand its real nature.

80

Paul Dessau

Dr. Giuseppe Becce

Arthur Honegger

Darius Milhaud

Part Three: Mechanical Interlude

A. Gramophone records as accompaniment

The year 1928 saw the first public appearance of the sound-film in the United States; in 1929 the sound-film—labelled as an American product—came over to Europe, and struck utter dismay into the hearts of all connected with the European film industry. Till that time, people had remained sceptical. True, they had heard of the extraordinary success achieved by Al Jolson's first big sound-film, *The Jazz Singer*, on the other side of the Ocean. And they had for quite a long time been aware of the experiments of the 'Tri-Ergon' people, the real inventors of the sound-on-film method which is now in general use, who were financed by the Tobis Company in Berlin. But, in spite of this, they considered the moment for the dictatorship of the sound-film had not yet arrived.

But when the great frenzy consequent on the sound-film invasion broke out in full force, and the technical factories were in vain trying to cope with all the demands made by studio and theatre for new apparatus, they lost their heads. A huge number of silent films lay there finished, others were just in the middle of production, hundreds of them still had to be paid for: were these to show a dead loss, like all the printed music in the stocks of the unfortunate publishers of film compilations? That would have spelt ruin for the whole European film industry. No effort was to be spared at least to postpone the coming of that 'evil', the sound-film; for, in the first place, the funds were not there for the reorganisation that was necessary and, in the second place, the technicians had not had time to adapt themselves to the needs of the new sound-industry. They had gained much electro-acoustical experience in their work on wireless and gramophone recording, but the sound-film confronted them with problems that were much more complex and varied.

In the sphere of film music, the state of affairs was even more catastrophic. Thousands of orchestral musicians were in the greatest danger of losing their livelihood. Inevitably the great demand for musicians in the heyday of the silent film had brought in its train a kind of boom in musicians. Amateurism flourished. Among the many thousands of ensemble players, only a small fraction could be called first-rate artists—a fact which did very much harm to the bona fide professionals.

And now the sound-film had arrived, the music became mechanised, and at once almost all film musicians were out of a job. Their associations lodged despairing protests with the public and the authorities concerned, but of course could do nothing at all to stem the tide of events. In every cinema the orchestra was the first item to be abolished, in favour of music produced electro-mechanically.

For without any delay, the public, crazy as it was over the sound-film, was offered something which pretended to be a 'sound-film', but in fact was nothing else than a silent film with mechanised music. The film forthwith hovered between silence and sound, and this artistic bastardy made the cinema loathsome even to the most patient of audiences. It is impossible to describe the lack of taste which was displayed in that period of about one or two years. European film production had completely lost its nerve in face of the assault made by the sound-film.

So orchestras were dismissed, and the orchestra pit at first covered over with a baize awning, as if with a shroud. Instead the house was filled with the strident tones of a loudspeaker braying out some gramophone reproduction. We have already seen that the idea of accompanying a film with mechanical music is as old as the film itself. Earlier experiments made by Edison, Lumière, and Messter had ended in failure because the technique of amplifier, loudspeaker, and microphone had not yet been developed. There are, of course, even to-day a host of technical problems to be solved connected with sound; there is in many cases considerable room for improvement in reproduction; nevertheless, men know how to make skilful use of the new instruments. But at that time, in 1929, they stood on the threshold of a new province, and did not know what artistic use to make of new technical developments.

Silent films were therefore illustrated with gramophone records: by means of certain synchronous couplings a higher degree of coincidence between sound and picture could gradually be achieved. In the beginning ordinary commercial records were used for the purpose: these were registered by an electromagnetic sound-box on an electrically driven playing-desk with several turn-tables, and passed over the amplifier to the loudspeaker. The playing-desk had to be so placed that its attendant could keep his eye on the screen the whole time. The operator of the mechanism was usually a cinema *chef d'or-chestre* who had lost his old position, and was now trying to apply his old theories of illustration to his records, as far as the proprietor of the cinema gave him any money for the purchase of records.

The individual turn-tables had a sound-overlapping plant, that is, the music on one record could be made to fade into the next, in a process analogous to the overlap of pictures. If a third turn-table was available, one could venture at certain junctures on an attempt to set some noise, perhaps even words, in counterpoint against the running music. These 'acoustic overlaps', technically produced by electrical resistances, formed the preliminary stage for a general technique of sound-overlap, which has today reached a high level of proficiency by mechanical means, namely by double exposure of the sound-strip. They were at that time necessary to preserve the illusion of continuous line in the musical accompaniment to some extent. For it was naturally undesirable that sudden interruptions should constantly occur, still less intervals between the different sections. Individual volume controls, one fitted to each turn-table, which enabled the dynamics to be graded at will, completed this system.

In this way an attempt was made by technical means to overcome the difficulties of the transitional stage when the device of modulations was not available, as had formerly been the case with the silent-film orchestra. In the end, a relatively advanced state of efficiency was attained, so that a skilful gramophone operator could produce the illusion, even on a sensitive ear, of a complete absence of musical cutting. In order to give the operator an exact idea of the cues for new records and their playing, an 'illustrative score' was prepared, containing details of

87

the exact length of film for each record. The correct
'entrance' of the record was devised as follows. The
film magazine in the projector set a numerator machine in motion. This machine was fitted on to the
playing-desk, and jumped one number on for every
foot of film that rolled off the magazine. It was
merely necessary to ascertain in the case of every
film the numbers of the feet on the film at which
acoustic overlaps had to be made, so that the operator
could act on the information given him by the cino-
meter (the measuring apparatus showing the film
lengths as they were rolled off) in connection with
the instructions on the illustrative score. Moreover it
was possible to carry out the dynamic directions indicated on the illustrative score with the aid of the
volume control.

Extraneous noise was reduced to a minimum, always excepting the low hum of the loudspeakers
(numbering on the average four), which even to-day
has not yet been eliminated. It must further be
noted that the quality of tone depended, as in the
case of the sound-film, not only on the sound-appar-
atus, but also on the acoustics of the individual
cinema.

For the illustration of a full-length film about
thirty or forty records were needed, all with the
same music on both sides. The ordinary records on
the market had proved increasingly useless for film

illustration, so these special *Kinothek* records were produced, containing cinema music exclusively. The principle of silent-film illustration was thereby transferred to record illustration. Cinemas budgeted for a collection of about three hundred records to give them a selection adequate for their constantly changing programmes. Some film companies delivered a printed list of records for use with their films; and this meant that they drew almost without exception on the products of one single firm.

Record manufacturers also had a hand in the chaos of styles which overtook the films as a consequence of this new principle of mechanical musical accompaniment. Some of them maintained publicly, in all seriousness, that the films which were illustrated with their products were sound-films. Special shots were made of speakers who were intended to 'double' any actors in the film whose mouth-movements were not clearly visible; and these helped to inculcate in the minds of the public an entirely false conception of the sound-film.

Part Three: Mechanical Interlude

B. The musicians disillusioned. Biographical retrospect

The fatal social consequences of this outbreak of mechanical music have already been mentioned. No less catastrophic were the dangers which threatened the development of the film from the artistic point of view. If creative musicians, as far as they occupied themselves with music for mechanical reproduction, cherished the hope, after the general decease of the cinema orchestra, that a new day for art was dawning, that original compositions would be required now that all former technical difficulties in sales and in performance had fallen away, they very soon saw all their hopes dashed to the ground. Nothing had changed. The illustration method was kept up; even fewer films than before required and received original accompaniment, apart from a few theme-songs. The film-producing companies pleaded the financial crisis which had arisen from the re-organisation due to the sound-film, and their one aim was to reproduce noises. Every door had to bang,

90

every step echo. Little matter whether synchronism was achieved or not!

So in this transitional period music experienced a considerable setback. It was gradually thrust more and more outside the cinema. Seldom, and only in big theatres, could concerts by live orchestras be heard. Not only the music played in the cinema, but the musical accompaniment of the film itself, became more and more neglected and depressed to a level which was far beneath that of the final silent-film period. All the efforts made by the record operators to maintain a certain artistic standard failed, if not on technical, then on financial grounds. No one could conceive why record reproductions should be given greater encouragement than an orchestra of live players, since in any case the sound-film had not yet arrived. Only in the very smallest houses, in which the musical performance had left room for improvement, were the records a blessing: at least one heard no more wrong notes. Even so, loud-speakers of inferior quality and certain attempts at reproduction without an amplifier did not always make the tone a perfect pleasure. . . .

The disillusionment of the musicians grew, and any of them worthy of the name retired. Apart from records with programme music, original compositions were no longer in demand; only the 'song hits' from the sound-films came more and more into fashion. The great theme-song craze began to cast its shadow before. . . .

And at this point, before we consider the sound-film proper, the main subject of this summary, it may be well to cast a brief glance back on the work of a few musicians to whom the silent film owed a good part of its artistic boom. We shall meet them for the most part again in the sound-film, and this is the best evidence that their qualities stood the strain and cruel hardship attendant on mechanical art. Their services to film music cannot be forgotten, because they live on in the history of film development.

We shall not attempt to anticipate biographical details, which are to be found in a chapter of the section on the sound-film, and we shall only specify the most important of these composers.

First, there was Giuseppe Becce, the first man to endow film music with a characteristic form of its own. Had it not been for his *Kinothek*, the musical illustration of silent films would have been still more problematical than was actually the case. He was also the first to compose original music, for a film called *Richard Wagner*, in the year 1913. His strength lay above all in the fact that he found the proper form and the characteristic musical formulae for the pictures. He was imitated so much all over the world that certain ornaments of his illustrations have become classic.

Next to him, the figure of Edmund Meisel, whose life was cut short all too prematurely, was and remains the most interesting of all. While Becce represented a musical epoch which was fast coming to an end, the new age was heralded by a man about twenty years his junior in Meisel. His expressionistic style, turning first and foremost on rhythm, was many stages in advance of the films for which he composed. His musical accompaniment for the Russian film *Battleship Potemkin* marked him out as a pioneer in film music. The film made a deep impression wherever it was shown, but there is no doubt that this impression was to no small extent enhanced by the music. It is significant that several European countries which allowed the film itself to pass the censor forbade the music to be played. Its really provocative rhythm was liable to lash the revolutionary instincts latent in audiences to boiling-point. It was reminiscent of that classical example of a revolution caused by music—the riot which resulted from the performance of Auber's *La Muette de Portici*. The rhythms which mark the departure of the mutinous ship, as the engines begin to move, have become famous, and have since been imitated countless times.

The music for the film *Potemkin* was Meisel's masterpiece. After that, he wasted his energy in useless musical experiments. *Berlin*, for instance, Ruttmann's documentary film, he ruined with his harsh atonalities. Later, shortly before the end of his brief career, he became a little more moderate, more by command of the industry than through any desire of his own. And his first attempts in sound-films, after which death overtook him, showed that he died with the silent film, in a kind of common destiny: apparently it was only with difficulty and reluctance that he managed to submit to the laws of the sound-film. Yet he remains as one of the strongest influences in film music.

Among the serious musicians who had already put their genius at the disposal of the silent films, we must further note Henri Rabaud with his music for *Le Miracle des Loups*, Arthur Honegger with his scores for the big Abel Gance films *La Roue* and *Napoléon*, as well as a smaller manuscript for *Faits divers* by Autant-Laura. Darius Milhaud had likewise written a film composition before sound-films arrived, the *Actualités*, which was first performed in 1928 at the Music Festival in Baden-Baden. Here we have really no score for one definite film strip, but a witty and charming persiflage on the stereotyped pictures of the weekly news-reel in the days of the silent film. This work, which was frequently performed (without the film), already evidenced Milhaud's eye for the essential requirements of film music.

In like manner, Arnold Schönberg's *Music for a*

Film Scene is occupied with the problem of silent-film music, inasmuch as the music was not an accompaniment for any existing film scene, but was meant to act merely as a type of film music. Of course, Schönberg's composition, written in the twelve-tone system, would hardly have been seriously considered for the accompaniment of a film, because it represents in the most abstract form a kind of treatise on the subject of film music which could be set for theoretical discussion in a concert-hall, but never be adapted or subordinated in practice to a film scene.

Paul Dessau wrote some film works before the sound-film era; these were superior to the abstract work by Schönberg in so far as they were absolutely applicable film music, and also were of an artistic standard which allowed their concert performance. Allusion is here made mainly to the suites for the Starewitch films, *The Magic Clock* and *The Enchanted Forest*. In these works the composer surpassed current film compositions in form, content, and style to a remarkable degree. Dessau, by the way, at this early date had already set quite a number of Walt Disney's silent cartoon films to music.

In America during the silent-film period, three musicians stood out above the rest: Riesenfeld, Zameznik, and Rappé, all three of whom did considerable work specially in the sphere of compilation

95

music and drills for cinema orchestras, without however having anything particularly new to show for
it.

Hosts of other film composers who lost their local
importance after the advent of the sound-film need
not be mentioned here, since it was our intention
only to give an outline of the silent-film period as
the historical preliminary to the sound-film.

Part Four: The Sound-Film

1. Sound technique
A. History of the technical developments

To understand the sound-film as we know it to-day, we shall find a short sketch of its history indispensable, as the seeds of future development are already conspicuous in it. The technique of the sound-film has now been put on such firm foundations that we may assume that the system will in the near future undergo no essential changes. In this respect we may already speak of a consolidation of sound-film technique. And since technique is here prerequisite to the artistic, above all the musical, consideration of the subject, musical experts, too, will appreciate an outline of the evolution of sound-film technique.

The American inventor Edison was the first man to occupy himself consciously with the sound-film. We have already noticed this in the first chapter of this book. His 'cinetophone', which he first brought out in the year 1899, consisted of three phonographs, reproducing the same sounds in order to achieve greater volume, but had as yet no synchronous coupling between picture and sound. It meant that a mechanic had to watch the film image behind the screen (which was transparent) and regulate the phonographs accordingly. Co-ordination between projection and sound-control was obtained by means of lamp signals. As these early sound-films only lasted a few minutes, the cylinders of the phonographs were only intended for a very short performance. Nevertheless, Edison thereby gave the first impetus to the treatment of the sound-film problem, and in the year 1905 came forward with an apparatus which was a considerable improvement. From that year we may date the actual development of specialized sound-film technique.

About 1900, Gaumont in France and, almost at the same time, Messter and Goldschmidt in Germany, combined films with records. A certain degree of synchronism was attained, of course, only mechanically, and not electrically implemented. It would lead us too far to recount all the single stages in this evolution, but the final phase was the American sound-on-disc method 'Vitaphone' and the German 'Lignose-Breusing'.

A quite different system of sound-reproduction was employed by the Frenchman Pineaud with the so-called relief process, in which the edge of the film was indented to record the sound and then played off at the touch of a style running along the notches. Pineaud built up his experiments on the work done by his countryman Hubert, who as early as 1870 had tried to make the relief process of picture telegraphy fit for practical use. Others to concern themselves with this problem were the German Reiss (the inventor of the microphone called after him) and the American Amstutz. Then, in the year 1902, Asam tried to produce a sound-film by making printed films swell up and playing them off with a gramophone needle, mica box, and so on. But the swelling caused difficulties in cases where sound and picture were on the same film strip.

Another system, similar to the relief method, was worked out by the Germans Bothe and Waltz, who roughened a phonogram strip and played it off in such a way that the pressure varied according to the roughness. And the so-called resistance film, which was used by Pfannhauser in 1904 and by Timm in 1911, also belongs to this category of experiments; here the different breadths of the resisting material were changed according to the varying sound-vibrations and consequently the galvanic resistance, so that an electric current underwent sound-rhythmical changes.

The real sound-on-film method, as it is exclusively

employed today, was first arrived at by the three German inventors, Vogt, Engel, and Massolle, who began their experiments about 1918 under the name of 'Tri-Ergon'. They, too, had forerunners: as early as 1880 the Englishmen Ayrton and Perry had sent a polarised light-ray through a coil charged by the sound-alternating current, in experiments for picture telegraphy. Besides them, various inventors, proceeding from the researches of Graham Bell (1893), Ruhmer (1900) and above all Duddel (1900), worked in the field of the recording of sound by light. Duddel had discovered that one could influence an electric ray by means of refractional currents, and Ruhmer made use of this discovery to construct his photographone, in which he projected the arc-light, vibrated by the sound-currents, on to a film. The German investigator Korn (1903) advanced further on the same path, but in contrast to Ruhmer he used, instead of the arc-light, a high-tension glow discharge between two electrodes. On this basis Schönfeldt (1919) and the Tri-Ergon group then built up their experiments.

As the history of the sound-film shows, the chief attention of all inventors was directed towards the improvement of the actual medium transposing the sound, the electric cell which developed more and more into the gas-discharge lamp. Besides the gas-discharge lamp experiments were also made with media which worked by light-technique, especially with the selenium cell. This changes its electric resistance under the influence of a beam of light falling upon it, but it has the disadvantage of a certain sluggishness, that is, it does not follow every light-vibration directly enough and is therefore less suitable for high sound-frequencies. The photo cell has gained a considerably greater currency in sound-film technique. It is a vacuous glass-tube, filled with certain alkalis, from which, by means of exposure to light, electrons charged in varying strengths, according to the strength of the exposure, are emitted.

About the same time as the practice of photographed sound, quite a different sound-process appeared, invented by Ludwig Blattner, and used for the first time for sound-films by Dr. Stille—the steel method, or magnet sound-method. It is based on the magnetisation of a steel wire or ribbon by a magnet charged by alternating current. By a special device the sound registered can be immediately 'rubbed out' again, without any change in the substance of the steel ribbon being caused thereby.

In spite of some advantages of this very economical method, which is especially suitable for teaching purposes, it failed to gain ground in the field of sound-film technique although it is still widely used by the B.B.C. Thus only two methods have proved themselves to be of practical utility, the

sound-on-film method and the *sound-on-disc* method;
and the latter was used only in the earliest period of
sound-films. To-day the sound-on-film process is completely dominant.

B. The sound-on-disc method

The sound-on-disc method gained ground all the more easily because in many cinemas apparatus for gramophone-record reproduction was already available, so that only the synchronisation instruments had to be built in. The first big American sound-films (*The Jazz Singer, The Singing Fool*) were sound-on-disc films. The sound-recording in this method proceeded as follows. The current-impulses from the microphone amplifier were recorded on wax discs. For this purpose, in the same way as in normal gramophone recording, the current-impulses from the amplifier were conducted to an electric sound-cutter. The variation from gramophone recording occurred above all in the size: the sound-film records had a diameter of 16 inches (contrasting with the 12 inches of the biggest gramophone records); in addition, they did not run at the normal speed of 78 revolutions per minute, but only did $33\frac{1}{3}$, which necessitated a playing-desk built with absolute precision and quite free from vibration. Another difference was that the needle mostly ran in performance from the middle of the disc outwards to the rim.

By means of a synchronous motor an exact connection was obtained between photographic camera and sound-camera. The speed of the revolutions therefore was in an exactly determined ratio to the speed of the crank gear in the photographic camera. The projecting machine for the sound-on-disc film consisted of a normal projector, from which a flexible coupling proceeded to revolve the appropriate gramophone record. On the latter an electrical pick-up was making contact, and conducted the weak currents with which it was charged over an amplifier to the loudspeaker. The difficulties of the transition from one record to the next were overcome as follows. Shortly before one record had finished playing, an electromagnetic coupling was switched on through a small metal cell attached at a suitable point in the perforation holes of the film strip running through the projector. This coupling in turn set the second record in motion by means of the flexible driving shaft mentioned above. When the latter had reached the proper speed, the first record stopped, and the operator could then change the records at his leisure and arrange their 'entrance' at the exact point indicated. It can be seen that in spite of a great degree of perfection this system still has much in common with the method of gramophone-record reproduction. Hence it did not hold its own for very long.

Some of the chief reasons for the complete transition from the sound-on-disc to the sound-on-film method were: the relatively quick wear and tear of the records; the danger of imperfect synchronism if the performance was not exactly timed; the impossibility of a speedy resumption of the performance if the film strip should happen to tear; the difficult cutting of the film and the general handicaps to its mobility.

C. The sound-on-film method

This method of making sound-films is based on a photographic fixing of the sound on the film strip. On a film of normal width, the sound is recorded at the side, on the inner surface of the perforation, either in lines (the variable-intensity system) or in zigzags (the variable-area system). After the cutting and editing of the film have been completed, the sound is situated 19 film frames in front of the picture to which it belongs, because in the reproducing machines the sound head is placed a corresponding distance below the picture-projection gate.

The sound-on-film process uses picture camera and sound-camera, both of which are synchronously coupled. Let us follow the currents of the sound-on-film camera, in which sounds are photographically registered. As they come from the microphone, they are first of all conducted to an amplifier and then to a gas-discharge lamp, which by means of a circuit is each time extinguished just at the moment when the current-impulses coming from the microphone arrive. So the gas-discharge lamp extinguishes itself many thousand times in a second, if the sound proceeding from the microphone is very high; with low tones, on the other hand, it only extinguishes itself a few times in the second. This is due to the fact that the so-called 'frequencies' are more numerous with high tones than with low ones. The term used for these frequencies is a unit of measurement—'cycles' or 'Hertz', after the great physicist of that name. High notes and hissing sounds count on the average anything up to 15,000 cycles, low tones reach about 40 cycles. These figures, it must be remembered, only represent the limit of what at the present day can in general be expected from recording cameras. The fact that new types of high-fidelity systems can go considerably further, both at the higher and the lower limit, promises greater facilities in recording and enrichment in melodic possibilities in the future.

The gas-discharge lamp is situated within the sound-recording camera in a box with a thin slit, in front of which an unexposed film strip runs past at exactly the same speed as the image-recording film in the picture camera. (Thus there are two films in synchronous motion at the same time, that in the picture camera and that in the sound-camera.) According to the number of frequencies and, in consequence, to the number of times the gas-discharge lamp goes out, there remain unexposed on the film strip here thinner and there thicker line-shaped areas and zigzags, so that in the end a kind of sound-writing becomes visible on the left side of the film, after the sound-strip is developed (this is done on the same basis as the development of the image strip). Picture film and sound-strip once completed, they are printed on top of one another by a special process. Beforehand, the sound-strip can be 'mixed' with noises, with music in counterpoint, and with speech—a job which has gained in importance as mixing and printing equipment have attained increased technical perfection.

The reproduction of the sound-on-film record is effected by inserting the film in a projector with a sound-registering system and exhibiting it in exactly the same way as a silent film. The sound-strip remains invisible during the projection, as it is masked off. The part carrying the sound-photography, as it runs through the sound-head, is illuminated by a carefully screened lamp which has a beam shaped in lines or dashes. The ray of light produced by it falls on to the photo cell, which gives off more or less current-impulses to the amplifier which is coupled to it, according as the sound-photography is made up of thin or thick lines (or zigzags). These current-impulses are then passed through the amplifier to the loudspeaker and thus converted into sounds.

D. Synchronisation

In the sound-film, there are in principle three kinds of recording: music taken in advance, music taken parallel with the picture photography, and music taken subsequently. The difficulty in moving sound-recording equipment about, when it is above all desirable that pure tone should be produced, has brought the recognition that it is much more economical to take important sound-sections of the film separately. Moreover, to-day, mixing technique is very highly developed, and, further, the cutting of the picture strip with the sound-strip is no longer a problem. In contrast to the early days of the sound-film, when the simultaneous taking of image and sound was considered absolutely necessary, to-day it is recognised that only certain parts of the film, especially dialogue, should be taken together with the picture, whilst the music in most cases is subsequently mixed into the picture. There are important financial reasons, and also technical and artistic considerations, in favour of this practice.

Musical synchronisation can be effected in one of two possible ways. The first, employed most frequently, proceeds as follows:

After the film in its final cutting and the composition are complete, the music is first rehearsed in the recording-room, and attention must then be paid to the fact that sound, which reacts differently in every room, must be reduced to one melodic common denominator. It is the sound-expert's business, either by changing the acoustics or by exact control of the sound according to a pattern of musical recordings taken in other rooms, to see that no differences in tone arise. (Cf. Part Four, Section 3, on acoustics and the problem of resonance in recording.)

Then the film is exhibited, and the conductor takes the music in relation to it, following precise signals for his entrance; and in the process the film strip intended for the sound-photography is running synchronously with the projector. He either sees his cues appear on the screen shortly before the scene in the picture begins, and then all he has to do is to follow the course of the picture; or he conducts by following the rhythm ribbon of a rhythmonome, or entrance signals of similar systems. It is very unusual for long sections to be taken one after the other. More than a few minutes are not synchronised continuously.

This process is in itself very simple. But, however great the efforts to render the work exact, accidents of all kinds, involving costly delays, can easily happen. The American 'play back' invention has the advantage of less danger, and accuracy more easily attained. It is the second alternative of musical synchronisation separate from the photography of the picture. It is now being used more and more extensively, above all in musical films. The fundamental principle consists in fixing the sound simultaneously on the film strip (*before* the picture is taken on it) and on a wax record: the latter is subsequently reproduced through a loudspeaker during the silent photography of the picture images: the photography is done by following the rhythm of the music. Let us assume for example that a ball scene has to be filmed. As the set essential for such a scene is very expensive, making it imperative that it should be completed as quickly as possible, silent photography is much cheaper than simultaneous sound and film photography, in which the least mistake would necessitate a repeat. So the music for the scene is taken on film and record together: then the record is reproduced through a loudspeaker, and the couples dance to its strains. After the picture strip is finished, it has only to be combined with the sound-strip, which has already been completed, to result inevitably in a perfect agreement of music with dance-rhythm. The incidental sounds of the ball could easily be added to the music by mixing. The two negatives were then 'married'. After the music is taken, the composer usually tests the individual sections once more at the hearing-desk by comparison with the score.

The technique of subsequent synchronisation is to-day based in all essential points on two systems, Blum's phonorhythmy (formerly termed rhythmography) and the Topoly system. The former is derived from Blum's rhythmonome, the main principles of which (and they have not changed since its first appearance) have been explained above (cf. Part Two, Section F, p. 66, *et seq.*).

By means of a rhythmoscope, the rhythmogram is produced on the basis of text or rhythm and recorded by a rhythmograph. This rhythm ribbon runs at a determinable speed—either in a box or else by projection on a screen—in front of the conductor, singer, or speaker. The performers then arrange their entrances the instant the ribbon passes a certain marking-line.

The Topoly system only differs in certain details from phonorhythmy, and is similar in principle. The most striking difference is the idea of using a rotating dial (called 'reel') instead of the ribbon rolling off a spool to mark the cues. The lines of text or music are set into circular staves on the reel, and these lines are arranged in squares, of which the area is identical with that of 10 film frames; a full circle of the dial (which is about a yard in diameter) corresponds with the turning of 1000 film frames. Naturally, the reel is timed to revolve in exact synchronism with the projector.

When the music (or the dialogue) has been finished according to the exact measurements of the film, its melodic line is recorded on ribbon or reel. Then the subsequent synchronisation can be begun without special difficulties in the studio. The conductor theoretically would no longer find it necessary, as formerly, to follow the silent film, shown simultaneously on the screen, as a control. This kind of subsequent synchronism is employed with the most signal success for doubling in foreign languages.

The actual sound-recording takes place before a series of microphones the number of which is not limited. (It has occurred in Hollywood that as many as twelve instruments were used for a single recording!) They are connected in the auditorium at a mixing-table, and from there are manipulated by the sound-recordist according to the requirements of sound-script. In this way it is possible for the most complicated sound-combinations to be produced and brought into plastic relief one against the other. To achieve the exact timing of the synchronism, some sound-recordists have at their disposal a

116

spark-writer, which automatically inscribes a spark on a measured paper film as the music or speech begins, so that all possible inexactitudes are eliminated by the mechanical control.

All these technical novelties, together with the fact that they are no longer tied to the enforced silence or to the bustle of the studio, have presented musicians with a host of possibilities. The experience gained in recording technique, and also the tone-combinations made possible by mixing, afford a new basis for musical activity, the full implications of which can scarcely be conceived. In connection with investigations into the part played by the various kinds of instruments, they may one day exercise a decisive influence on the whole art of music. We shall revert to these problems once more in a later section.

2. Music and the Sound-film
A. The 'theme-song' craze

We were unable to avoid an outline of the growth of the sound-film from the technical side, as this new form of art cannot be discussed in its artistic implications without prior knowledge of its technique. And now, having followed the history of the film through three decades, we come to the point where we consider the short period of the sound-film's development from the aesthetic aspect in general, and in particular from the practical artist's point of view. The sound-film has already, despite its youth, passed through several stylistic periods, without coming any nearer to the discovery of its own real appropriate style.

We have already mentioned the embarrassment caused to European film production as a result of the first American sound-films. We have also seen the lowering of musical standards in a short transitional period of mechanical experiment. When finally the technical character of the sound-film began to crys-

118

tallise, after the sound-on-disc film was abandoned and the sound-on-film method, with its greater possibilities, became the rule, then very gradually the artistic form of the sound-film began to follow in the train of a technique that had outstripped it by far.

In the beginning every noise was a matter of rejoicing, and no opportunity was missed of making it heard. Experiments were being made with the effect of acoustics on sound-volume, and brains were racked to find out what kind of sound-production would be most suitable. At such a time the actual form of the sound-film—and therefore of its music—remained a controversial topic. The first period of the purely noise films was followed by undiluted dialogue films and sound-film operettas. The dialogue film, first created in Hollywood, soon came to an end for the time being: the language difficulty precluded export, and post-synchronism in the present sense of the term was not yet known. As a result, a return was made to music, but admittedly only in a very negative way. The dullest and most stale devices of operetta were transplanted into the cinema, and the plague of the 'song hit' infected the world's film industries.

In the last year of silent films, such theme-songs had already begun to be tacked on to a few individual films, to gain increased propaganda for them by means of records and other methods of publicity.

119

This germ of the theme-song spread with terrible rapidity, became an epidemic, and systematically disintegrated the sound-film. For its style has been totally destroyed by this craze, always excepting the genuine musical comedies that have been filmed. Thus serious plays became operettas and drama changed into farce. The dramatic texture was torn out of even the neatest manuscript, and still is sometimes, though nowadays far more care is taken to motivate these songs properly.

The theme-song broke the tension at the most important points in the film, because it held up the action. And the film must never linger without reason: requiring, by its very nature, incessant motion. The song hit with its usually stupid and insipid text, lowered the general level of the early sound-film even below that in the period of mechanical interludes. In consequence of the inevitable mass production of songs, a veritable *song-hit boom* occurred, until it was barely possible to distinguish between one number and the next. And it came to this: all the money which was taken as a result of these theme-songs to fill up the empty coffers of the film-producing companies, proved to be but a Greek gift: the public tired of the sound-film.

It would be a fallacy to assume that the beginning of the sudden film crisis in all the producing countries of the world was solely due to economic causes.

120

For there are examples to prove that good and interesting films pay their way. The crisis derived above all from the fact that the insipidity and lack of taste displayed in most films knew no bounds and finally frightened the public from the cinema. (The Protectionist policy of certain countries almost succeeded in making the crisis a permanency, in spite of the upward tendency which later ensued. . . .)

So, in consequence of the song-hit craze, the film's true character became more and more obscured. There was hardly any difference of style between serious drama and comedy. This lax conception of art in the minds of many producers coincided with the tendency to make only such films as would please if possible all tastes and all classes of people. Not only in their form, but also in their content, were the films intended to give something to satisfy every taste. But at a time when opinions everywhere in the world are more sharply divided than ever before on the subject of the life men should lead, opportunism of this kind very soon reaches the end of its tether. Lack of character, which in the artistic sense is identical with absence of style, must be banished at all costs from the scenarios.

It is abundantly clear that film music had a hard struggle in this age of formlessness, mental shallowness, and complete artistic chaos. At last it had come to pass that compiled music was abandoned and original compositions were ordered. But what compositions! It was only after producing companies had learnt their lesson through bitter experience, and thanks to the strenuous efforts of all those who had the furtherance of the sound-film and its artistic development at heart, that at last some other schools of thought made themselves heard, and artists were permitted to search for new forms for the musical sound-film. For it became more and more obvious that the sound-film *had* to be furnished for long stretches at a time with music, and that purely dialogue films had to be strictly limited in number.

B. Dangers of background music

At this point, a few words will not be amiss on the subject of a new fashion, that of 'background' music, which is threatening to do great harm. Just as once the sound-film song hit ruined the whole structure of many films, so now a pernicious habit of 'mixing' music behind a scene, without any particular motive or connection, has already had quite a number of unpleasant consequences.

To give an example. A pair of lovers speak of their feelings for one another; or a tearful parting is enacted; or a dead man is being mourned. The list can be enlarged at will: any emotional moment in life is appropriate. Suddenly—no one can tell why—a violin starts sighing out some tearful phrase. Result —a terrible strain on the lachrymal glands. It is an abuse of music to obtain with it a dramatic effect which should be achieved in any case, provided the situation be well founded, well acted, and well staged.

123

Or an educational film is being shown. All the while, the commentator's voice speaks words of wisdom, more or less. The intelligence of the public is still rated very low indeed by most companies, and the producers of the film are afraid that musical ground-tones alone will not suffice to keep the interest of the audience alive. All through the film, therefore, can be heard, proceeding from an undefined source, soft but confused music. As we watch, we do not quite know whether to listen to the melody or the commentator. If the latter makes a pause, the music at once sounds louder; when he begins again, it becomes a shade more soft, but does not cease to be obtrusive.

This vulgar straining after effect has unfortunately become noticeable even in big films, in scenes, moreover, where there could be no possible justification for it, either in the form of an orchestra playing behind the action of the film or of a radio instrument appearing in the picture. It has recently spread with painful rapidity. The most impressive of sound-films have suffered greatly as a result of a fashion which has not always as much as good intentions, and almost invariably is fraught with evil.

The genesis of background music presumably can be traced to the attempts at musical films which we describe and analyse below as 'musicals without much dialogue'. But in the course of its 'development' the part which incidental music ought to play in a sound-film was forgotten. There are in reality only a very few occasions which would justify a use of 'illustrative' background music; still less, a mixture of speech, music, and noises (noise 'sets'). The dangers of background music are indeed very great.

If it is true that the film, *even* in its purely commercial products, is supposed to be a form of art with a function to perform—if it is true that this art calls for respect, inasmuch as it has won a following in the best parts of society—then it is at last time to put a stop to these barbarous habits. *Background music, in the sense in which it has hitherto mostly been employed, is nothing else but a return to the primitive film.*

The dramatic possibilities of sound in present-day films and the uses and applications of music are numerous enough. Music as transition, music as the object of sound-events—yes, even as entertainment or an element of good cheer—will still serve its purpose. But, if it is employed to strain after effects which the film itself cannot induce, then it degrades the film and itself. It becomes a makeshift like the inevitable harmonium of thirty years ago, which was played alternately with the piano to compete with the loud rattling sound made by the projector in those days of naïve blood-and-thunder films.

We must not forget that the functions of music

with the sound-film are of a fundamentally different character from its functions with the silent film. At that time it did not have to hold its own with the voices which to-day issue from the loudspeaker, and so it served a real purpose as an active acoustical ally. Though it belonged to the film, it was not a part of it; whereas now it is an integral part of the sound-film. In other words, music must have its meaning. There must be good reasons for its sound to be heard. But background music is generally just as purposeless or even nonsensical as so many song hits proved to be.

It would be in the interests of the producing companies themselves to banish this execrable feature as soon and as radically as possible from their films. It is perhaps less conspicuous than the theme-song craze, but hardly less harmful.

Let us now consider a few 'musical' film forms, derived from the traditions of the theatre, opera, operetta, and even the concert-hall. Our object is to see how far they are applicable to the sound-film.

C. Various forms of 'musical' films

Operetta

The adoption of the old type of stage operetta, which we see for example in the classical Viennese form, was attempted—with and without alterations—by sound-film producers. Results have shown that this type, in its existing form, is of no use at all for sound-films. The old popular drama with musical accompaniment tends with each passing year to assume more and more of the status of a museum-piece, because its public is disappearing along with the differentiation in social classes, and its chief theme, the contact of middle-class environment with the 'higher' walks of life, no longer fits into the social structure of our day. The operetta, on the other hand, is more adaptable. It has developed from the ancient mime right down to the standard Viennese form: so why should it not, at least in some of its elements, be available for the sound-film? There were two possibilities in this direction: the musical *cabaret-revue* and *musical theatre*.

The revue is nothing else but pure spectacle with music. In it the appeal is much more to the eye than to the ear, whereas in film operetta music is of paramount value, laying down the whole rhythm for the course of the plot and the dynamics of the form. The music for a film revue, on the other hand, plays formally and dramatically a trivial part, since here spectacular effect in the scenery is far more important than any well-defined form; at most there are fixed dance-rhythms and the tempo is given. There are plenty of opportunities for introducing song hits, which have at least some modest meaning in this context as dance-songs. But as soon as the dramatic form becomes more complicated, the proper sphere of revue is already left behind us, and we enter the realm of operetta—or at least what, for want of a better and more appropriate description, we label such in its adaptation to sound-films.

Film operetta, a form of sound-film which both artistically and commercially has about the best prospects of all, will in its new guise have to go back to antique mime, which was a kind of musical stage-show, with musical and choric climaxes on the one hand, and points of emphasis expressed by dance on the other. Thus it is specially suited for stylised versions of its basic form. ('Stylised' is not here used in

128

The Brothers Karamazov by Fedor Ozep. (Departure of the prison train for Siberia.) Examples of Karol Rathaus's music face pages 158 and 176

A Nous la liberté by René Clair (March of the Workers). Maurice Jaubert wrote the score

the sense of a modern opera production. For the film is an art which is close to reality and which gains more naturalism as its technique becomes more highly developed. Sound-films certainly achieved greater naturalism, as against the silent films, through the addition of sound—which is yet another reason why film principles should be revised.)

The nearest approach to the sound-film operetta is the dumb show, by virtue of the causal connection between its music and its action.

Wilhelm Thiele's film, *Chemin du Paradis* (in Germany *Drei von der Tankstelle*), with W. R. Heymann's musical accompaniment, was one of the first examples of what a modern mime, transferred to the medium of the sound-film operetta, should be. Heymann's music is simple and popular, but without any special *sound-film* characteristics; and the factor which makes the film significant in the framework of our analysis—absolute coincidence of rhythms and forms in music and picture, and the new construction in dumb show—is in this case derived more from the director's than from the composer's art.

It is not generally known that René Clair was influenced by Thiele in developing the technique of matching the plot of his picture to the rhythms of the music. Clair studied sound-film technique in Berlin at a time when Thiele was already experimenting with film operetta technique, and later produced

Sous les Toits de Paris was produced in Paris. In England, too, Thiele's influence was considerable. The success of *Sunshine Susie*, one of the most financially satisfactory British films, can undoubtedly be traced to the original version made by Thiele, although his name was not associated with the English film.

Furthermore, Friedrich Holländer has shown in some experiments of his how the music has to grow organically out of the rhythm of the pictures and their action. If it then expands into a song, that is, if the continuous line passes from the movement motivated by the happenings of the plot into music (which itself, after merely determining the rhythm, ends in a compact song-form), then one can endorse the *raison d'être* of the theme-song, because it is dramatically premised.

The sound-film operetta, above all, has its laws, in conformity with which dialogue and song, periods of repose and action alternate and advance to a climax; so the music in it has to play a special part, which far transcends that of mere illustration. Dramatic incidents become the starting-point of thematic material, or the musical accompaniment of a silent passage harks back to or lays the stage for some rhythmic episode. Music in connection with this kind of film mime fulfils far more decisive duties than music which gives a revue atmosphere or is merely illustration to silent scenes. It transforms, in a word, the whole plot into a rhythm of sound. It multiplies the simple gesture until the dance, as the highest conception of rhythmic action, is reached.

Such a form is just as inconceivable without integral music as the old-fashioned operetta transplanted on to the screen. Yet attempts were made to 'arrange' banal libretti for the films. Since it was impossible to achieve this with any sense, in most cases indescribable stupidity bid defiance to every law of reason, and there was scarcely any practical justification for even one of the musical climaxes, for the theme-song.

The artistic worth of the sound-film operetta depends on the purity of its style. The man who makes a hash of all fundamental rules, by simply cutting theme-songs into other forms of sound-film, fails to create an operetta, or a musical play (which last can hardly be distinguished from the operetta, where the sound-film is concerned). Here we must point out that in this connection the words 'play' or 'theatre' are not meant to indicate the stage, the laws of which are still farther distant from the film than the silent is from the sound-film. In consequence, it seems to us that the photographed theatre, which does not come within the scope of our investigations, is no suitable form for the film, and all efforts in this direction, exemplified mainly in

France, find themselves of necessity in a cul-de-sac. Every thinking cinema-goer to-day knows that the film has its own laws, any violation of which is only too evident. . . .

There are no opera libretti to be found in existing stage literature which are suited to the sound-film, and, as a corollary, no really characteristic film music. Musical plays, too, written for stage performance, are with difficulty transferable to the screen and the loudspeaker; the *Opéra de quat' sous* (in German the *Dreigroschenoper*, a modern version of *The Beggar's Opera*) is a classic example of a stage play which was a success in that form, but did not prove equally suitable on the screen. Of the countless stage operettas which have been filmed, there probably is not one which could stand up to a serious artistic analysis. One must therefore work at new material in conformity with the special requirements of the sound-film, and this must be done in co-operation with the composer, whose share in the task must in no way be subordinated to the author's.

Again and again those responsible for a film have to face the question whether, even after a good rhythmic modulation, the culminating theme-song does not cause a lessening of the tension. In a film the music must never be allowed to become stationary or to hold up the general movement. It must flow on its even course, even when the visual images are apparently standing still. Perhaps that is the reason why an adaptation of the musical stage that is all too faithful in style to its original, the basis of which is actually its musical culmination in a solo or ensemble number, can only with the greatest caution be made for the screen. There is hardly anything which can imperil the effect of a film more than a stoppage in the action. Its movement cannot, perhaps, be ever in ascent or descent, but it must maintain its even flow.

So the musician has a very acceptable and responsible task in this new form of film operetta, for the success of the whole depends on his dramatic insight. But even the cleverest music cannot counterbalance bad construction in the scenic direction of a film.

Straight drama, with little dialogue, and musical accompaniment

This was a development of the stylised sound-film operetta. An early form of it appeared for the first time in one of the original German sound-films, the *Land ohne Frauen* (Country without Women). This film soon fell into oblivion amidst all the hubbub of the song-hit epidemic and owing to the lack of understanding evinced even by the press. The film with music, and little dialogue, that is familiar today, had an almost perfect example in René Clair's *Sous les toits de Paris*. If the German sound-film had appeared too early, in advance of its time, at least Clair's was understood well enough to be taken as the starting-point of a new school in style.

Clair's films created a film type which was adapted (in a somewhat altered form) even by the Americans, and which reached the peak of perfection in Wanger's *President Vanisher*. In this sound-film the purified form of film song was used for the first time —partly to a purpose that was almost *Leitmotiv* in character, and partly as an outline of atmosphere which again approached the old illustrative music.

We may assert that the success which attended this kind of film rather tended to lessen the number of pure dialogue films. Film directors learnt how to use a theme-song, if they could not avoid resorting to this device in their work. Since that time, too, they have sometimes made an attempt to bring the commercial requirements of their film production within a framework which was artistically tolerable. René Clair's films were the beginning of a more agreeable epoch'in sound-films.

The musical form of such films is very often connected with that of operetta, without however adopting the actual elements of the latter. It has wider functions, because the action is not built up exclusively on music, nor absolutely on one defined rhythm, but is rather based, without being stylised, on atmosphere and realism. The abandonment of everything stylised may be regarded as the most important difference—which, if recognised, will save film-creators from a mixed style.

The musical accompaniment in a film which is a play with little dialogue appears for long stretches at a time to play the part played by illustration in silent films. But here we have the essential distinction between musical accompaniment in silent and in sound films: in the latter, there are never more than relatively short lengths of film running 'silent' and having no other sound than the music, whereas the whole of a silent film must inevitably be illustrated. Sound-films need no illustration, but their music has to be the psychological advancement of the action. While therefore we may characterise silent-film music as descriptive, or the music of a sound-film operetta as a near approach to dumb show, the music accompanying the scenes which are without dialogue in a sound-film is neither illustrative nor mimetic. It is an altogether new mixture of musical elements. It has to connect dialogue sections without friction; it has to establish associations of ideas and carry on developments of thought; and, over and above all this, it has to intensify the incidence of climax and prepare for further dramatic action.

It can be seen that the task of writing music to fulfil these functions is much more difficult than that of writing for the silent films, in which one could escape a more profound interpretation by using the old catchphrases of descriptive music. Such sound-film compositions are invariably original music: when the mechanical interlude between silent and sound-films had once come to an end, the use of existing music was finally abandoned, and, although at first this mainly meant the song hit and its variations, composers did at last begin to exercise an increased influence.

The significance of such passages without dialogue (but not always without incidental noises) which were accompanied by music led—together with a general aversion to the increasing prevalence of dialogue, and also exigencies of production—to a strong temporary avoidance of the spoken word. The film *Marie*, by Paul Fejos, in which scarcely a single word is spoken, is the consummation of this movement. In the music accompanying this film the illustrative elements of the silent film actually appear once more. Charlie Chaplin's new film, *Modern Times*, falls into the same category. Even more consciously than was the case with *Marie*, Chaplin adapted his film to silent-film technique. He makes himself responsible for the composition of the musical accompaniment with his own signature. We may safely say that the music was hardly composed by him: he probably only gave his musical assistants

136

pointers regarding the effects at which he aimed. Unfortunately, his musical taste does not reach the high level of his mimetic art. The musical accompaniment to *Modern Times* is banal and superficial, and, to put it bluntly, silent-film melodrama which has long since gone out of fashion. Such films are really no longer true sound-films: for by a sound-film we mean not only a film that is taken according to the technology of sound-pictures; on the contrary, technique is merely the *sine qua non* of the artistic form, which has its basis in a perfect balance of scenic and sound dramaturgy. And by 'sound' we mean not merely music, but the epitome of human and natural sounds.

Straight films without much dialogue and accompanied by music will probably have as important a future as operetta films. The case of *Sous les toits de Paris* was evidence that a deeply studied sound-picture form makes versions in several languages unnecessary, and that the whole world understands such films. A few translations of the dialogue cut into the film are quite sufficient. Again, if versions in foreign languages were needed, such films with little dialogue were produced more cheaply and easily. Apart from that, it does no harm if the visual element in a film is thrust to the foreground and the acoustical sacrificed. As the film remains first and foremost a visual art, the opposite relation, that of overemphasis of acoustical effects, should in fact be avoided. Music has to play the part of a levelling influence, and musicians should always realise that the future belongs to the sound-film that is enriched by music (leaving aside documentary sound-films).

Nevertheless this kind of sound-film cannot be described as pure musical film. But the cultivation of the musical film has gained all the greater importance, inasmuch as opera and concert in their present form attract a public that is ever growing smaller in numbers, until one day even this small circle will be swallowed up in the changes that are everywhere taking place in the stratification of society. When this happens, the existing forms of sound-film will not suffice for the cultivation of music: even to-day they no longer fulfil the requirements of all those who can no longer afford the luxury of regular visits to concerts or opera.

But it is not only a problem of money which is hastening the decline of present-day forms of musical activity: the conditions of common musical experience on which existing forms of musical activity were built up have disappeared. As a great multitude of people, voluntarily or compulsorily, now go without artistic entertainments of high cultural standing, the film, as the popular art *par excellence*, has the social duty of taking up the thread where the bourgeois culture of the nineteenth century left off. Wireless alone is not sufficient to maintain musical culture; moreover, it uses up its power by the enormous amount of its musical transmissions. The film, however, with its visual capacities, meets man's primitive desire not only to hear, but also to see—a fact which should greatly facilitate the development of a specific musical film form.

Operatic sound-film—sound-film opera

The attempt was made, some time after the first sound-films had appeared, to produce operatic sound-films, that is, film versions of scenes in opera, as they are enacted in the opera-house, taken on the sound film strip. Social reasons were adduced for this development: the man in the provincial town and the simple villager, it was said, should in his cinema obtain the same artistic impression that formerly was vouchsafed only to the population of big cities with large musical institutions. With these ideas of advancing the general welfare of mankind were naturally combined very real commercial motives. But those who made this experiment did not reckon with the peculiar nature of the sound-film. For the film version of an opera performance is impossible and intolerable. Those elements for which on the operatic stage even to-day allowance is made, under the influence of the personalities of live artists, must on the screen have an insipid, ridiculous, and anachronistic effect. The camera brings the singer's pathos much too close to the spectator; a close-up of a photographed high C, on which the distorted face of the tenor, with wide-open mouth, is to be seen, at once destroys the effect of even the most beautiful melody and resolves it into laughter or even disgust. The unreal world of opera and the naturalistic film have nothing whatever in common.

Even more than in the living theatre the lack of constant action would disturb the effect: opera is static, film dynamic. An alternation between detailed close-ups and panoramic effects would only be possible to a limited extent, perhaps only in pantomimic situations with considerable dramatic action. The length-dimensions of an opera could only with difficulty be made to coincide with those of a film; abbreviated arrangements for film purposes would with most works inevitably destroy the line of the original score.

The operatic stage keeps its spell only when it is symbolically removed from the audience by the orchestra pit: thus it retains the air of 'once upon a time', the element of the extraordinary. Opera walks on buskins, the film on ordinary low heels. The dramatic direction of opera differs from that of the film so fundamentally that an adoption of opera by the film can only take the form of an allusive narration. One has often enough seen opera scenes in a film used to illumine the capacities of some hero or heroine, some star of song.

On the other hand, modern opera production can in certain circumstances fit the film very well into the total complex. Such a use of the film took place on the occasion of the Berlin première of Milhaud's *Christopher Columbus*. The film there played the part of a psychical reflection of the hero Columbus, whose feelings were symbolised in concrete occurrences shown on a concealed screen in the background of the stage. The silent film needed for the purpose was not composed of already existing films, but was turned for the occasion.

But arrangements of operas for the film have their all but inescapable pitfalls. Attempts have been made (most of them remain unexecuted) to transform some operatic plots which are especially striking from the pictorial point of view: for instance, *The Flying Dutchman, Carmen, Aïda,* and some others. The intention was to present single sections of the operas for hearing only, and not to enact them; concrete scenic occurrences were to be adapted to the music. The Dutchman's narration in the First Act, for example, would not only have shown the man himself, but would also have conveyed everything that he recounted. That there would be no lack of

141

naturalistic effects is quite clear; at that time it was regarded as a necessity that Lohengrin's swan should actually swim away down the Schelde, that Carmen should really display her charms in Seville and nowhere else, or that Aïda and Radames should sing their duet at the foot of a real pyramid or beside the true Nile.

All these extremely naïve projects were considered in all seriousness only a few years ago. But one soon realised that there was no sense in approaching the musical film from this primitive point of view. Even with fundamentally film-characteristic arrangements, such as we have seen in connection with the filming of Smetana's *Bartered Bride* or Rossini's *Barber of Seville* and a few other experiments of a like nature, it was evident how extraordinarily dangerous it could be to disregard the artistic rules of the sound-film and to forget in the process that well-known works of operatic literature have become rigid conceptions which may not be touched by the film.

One cannot make a sound-film a continuous composition, like an opera. And this basic law implies a negation of the operatic sound-film in itself. In this way we arrive at the sound-film opera, a concept which is contradictory in itself and therefore can give rise to grave misunderstandings. It would be better simply to say musical film, for the musical sound-film should denote nothing else. The elements of opera are in no respect applicable to it. Every adoption of these elements would stand in the way of the creation of a characteristic form of musical film.

In this connection the question arises whether the different kinds of film styles may be classified according to the traditional distinctions of the theatre, whether we can discriminate between tragedy, comedy, farce, musical comedy, operetta, and opera.

On principle, a classification of the film is needed for a clear exposition of its various styles. It is true that the gay and serious forms overlap far more than in the theatre, and the Lessing laws of dramatic construction are no longer valid. Nevertheless, we can keep apart films of entertainment, as a purpose in itself, from those which pursue some single idea in realistic or imaginary form. The purely entertaining films will be composed mostly of elements of comedy or operetta, or present themselves as so-called society films; in films with ideas, which have an artistic value, a distinction is the easier, inasmuch as they represent a form with a concentrated style which from the beginning was planned according to a definite principle. Only to keep film style comparatively pure does a classification of the film appear of importance.

Among musical films we should have to distinguish operetta films (including revue and cabaret films) from films with little dialogue accompanied by music (including stage plays with music) and from films which are intrinsically musical: for the last no form has as yet been discovered, and we have, with all possible vehemence, just rejected as mere cliché the name of opera for them. The evolution of these purely musical films is faced with the difficulty of finding a form which will not overlap on adjacent styles.

There had been so far, here and there, individual passages in certain films which foreshadowed such an ideal musical film. There can hardly be any doubt, the ideas of the film industry being what they are, that this ideal can only be realised in rare cases. Its future form will probably be a fusion of song (solos and *small* combinations), orchestral music, extraneous noises, and perhaps a little of the spoken word: that is, it will bring the most varied elements of the histrionic arts and musical forms under one roof. Only the musical film as such could include those melodramatic effects, which so often in dialogue films and even in documentary films obscured the words and made the spectators nervous. To play music as an accompaniment to a text, without a definite justification of meaning, is one of the most criminal blunders possible in sound-direction.

The systematic articulation and development of the purely musical film remains one of the most important problems of the sound-film of the future.

Dr. Karol Rathaus

Michael Spoliansky

Eric Sarnette

Hanns Eisler

Concert films

The film is first and foremost a visual, the concert an acoustical method of presentation. Can one intelligibly fuse these two different forms of art into one another? Should one do it, on principle?

Undoubtedly yes. Concert films have many functions to fulfil, which increase their significance far beyond their scant length of film strip (so far this type has only run to short films of a few thousand feet in length). They are an instrument of culture in so far as they bring great music, interpreted by great conductors, or with the authentic conception of well-known composers, to every place where people have had no opportunity of attending a concert. Their music may be potted but it is worth while. For it must be emphasised once again that all the capacities of the gramophone record and wireless are not adequate to arouse any really profound interest and understanding for serious music in the great majority of their hearers. Music heard like this is an abstraction, and the majority of people, being unaccustomed to conscious efforts of thought, react more easily to concrete presentation, that is, to *pictures* of every kind. Hence the world-wide success of the film; hence the increased number of illustrations in the newspapers and many similar phenomena. The intellectuals always overlook the fact that the man-in-the-street, unaccustomed to thinking, prefers something he can see, and therefore grasp quickly, to conceptions or sounds which as such are not to be apprehended without effort.

Whilst concerts and their performers can be transplanted to every place in the world through the medium of the sound-film, concert films have also great value as archives, less indeed for ourselves than for future generations. To realise what a tremendous blessing they might be, we have only to imagine what a treasure we should possess, had there been in earlier times any means of handing down to posterity the great masters of music in sound-pictures. We could watch Beethoven, Wagner, and other famous masters conducting, and so come to understand their artistic personalities better than in the best of biographies.

Last but not least, concert films offer an essential resource in the sphere of preliminary programmes, which in any case leave room for improvement both in quality and quantity. This kind of film should not be limited, as hitherto, to the usual well-known items under famous conductors, but all great composers ought to be systematically induced to conduct one of their works. In this way the cultural and historical value of the concert film would be augmented, and the whole idea of the concert film, which was carried out for the first time in 1932 in

Berlin, would be made more interesting, valuable, topical, and popular.

One definite method of taking such films has already been evolved. The scenario is written on the basis of the score. The camera must be fairly mobile and watch not only the conductor, but the various groups of instruments as well; a continuous view of the whole orchestra would conflict with the intrinsic nature of the film, which seeks incessant motion. It is not so simple to find a logical line of development for this sort of film in terms of musical rhythm and visual analysis. An indiscriminate roaming among the orchestra on the part of the picture camera is, of course, quite senseless. The sections, groupings, and movements in the score must be translated to the same degree into the editing and given their full value in the film.

There follows a short passage out of the scenario of the first of these concert sound-films, Rossini's *William Tell* overture, conducted by Max von Schillings a year before his death. It is the second section of the overture, the first Allegro (time: *alla breve*, 4/4):

Bars 1-44:   Focussing on the strings. Small groups of string-players visible in the picture.

Bars 45-79:   The camera travels from right to left, until the whole orchestra is seen.
The conductor seen as from the orchestra, alter-

147

	nately in profile and *en face*, interspersed with pictures of the trombonists now and then.
Bar 80:	A close-up of the cymbal-player sitting in the top seat of the orchestra, as he rises and strikes the cymbals against each other.
Bars 81-83:	Close-up of the conductor as from the audience.
Bars 84-116:	The camera slowly travels backwards, and the orchestra gradually moves farther and farther into the distance.
Bars 117-128:	Long-distance shot of the orchestra. As the picture fades away the music dies away with it.

In this brief 'scene' we can see the attempt to achieve a coincidence between rhythm, musical form, visual requirements of the film, and the meaning of the music. With more experience and more interesting music, increased visual possibilities will offer themselves.

The pictures are best taken in acoustically faultless concert-halls, in which any sound-absorbing foci can be eliminated by drapings of cloth. This also makes all decorative settings unnecessary. The picture cameras (there are several of them) have to be made as mobile as possible by means of rail-tracks and judicious positioning, in order to give the editor afterwards the most ample and varied opportunities when he treats the film. A single day is as a rule sufficient for the rehearsals and turning of a concert film about 1000 feet in length.

Sound cartoon films

This form of sound-film offers at the present time far the best and most perfect impression of the musical film, since it combines music, song, words, and incidental noises with the pictures into one stylistically finished whole in absolute rhythmic uniformity. Walt Disney created the classic films of this category. His Mickey Mouse films and the 'Silly Symphonies', most of them recently in colour, were worthy representatives of their type—a proof of the great art by which unity of sound and picture can be attained. The way in which idea, movement, and music were blended in them into a perfect harmony, gave an aesthetic pleasure which was renewed with each showing of such a film; it was also a pointer in the problem of how sound-films should be construed. The great popularity enjoyed by these films all the world over is due, not only to the brilliantly conceived figure of Mickey and to the clever parody and characteristic portrayal of human feelings by these animals in human form and garb, but also to the perfection of the framework in which the creatures of Disney's imagination moved.

We have spoken of these works of art in the past tense, because latterly these films, though pictorially as attractive as ever, musically no longer always attain the same standard of excellence. The fact that

149

a theme-song such as that in the *Three Little Pigs* gained a world-wide success evidently gave the producers the unhappy idea of always supplying the sound-cartoons with their own 'song hits' from then on. The inevitable consequences followed: a musical decline set in, in these very films of Disney's, which at once made the general effect shallow and insipid. If it is true to say that to-day the public is getting a little tired of these films, and that the element of colour is being flogged for all it is worth to dispel that feeling of satiety, then this fact can be placed first and foremost to the account of musical laxity. Only recently have the successful cartoons *Music Land* and *Mickey's Grand Opera* again evidenced a spirit of originality in the musical element which for a time had been lost.

The musical accompaniment of the Disney films, while in point of synchronous technique faultlessly made in every respect, is in its content of no account. The contrast with the films of his first period, which proved for the first time how truly great an art the sound-film can be, when it is rightly understood, is altogether striking.

To take their place, a considerable number of artists have mastered the cartoon-film form. They felt very rightly that in this field they were for the present offered the greatest opportunities of carrying out their artistic ideas—at any rate greater than in the

First page of Arthur Honegger's score for the cartoon
film by Maserel-Bartosch, *The Idea*. Facsimile of the
original MS. (Please note the use of the Ondium
Martenot in the first line of the score.)

studios of film companies who put commercial considerations before all else. The three most interesting types of these films may be briefly outlined as follows.

Following Franz Maserel's scenario and to the accompaniment of Honegger's music, the painter Bartosch created *The Idea*, a cartoon film with a pacifist theme. On another page of this book, a specimen of Honegger's score is to be found. Bartosch cut the figures out, painted them in black and white, and gave their limbs mobility. He photographed them through a table consisting of several layers of glass, so that, by the independence of the background and the differences in dimensions caused by the various strata of glass plates, he obtained a comparatively vivid plastic effect. Honegger's music was taken after the film had been completed, by approximately the same process as that by which the Disney films are synchronised. That means: the length of the film and of its individual scenes are accurately measured in co-operation with the composer, the score is constructed accordingly, so that the simple act of subsequent synchronisation causes no difficulties whatever and can be carried out with complete precision.

A quite different procedure is to be observed in Alexeiev's *Night on the Bare Mountain*. Here the artist used an already existent score of Moussorgsky's from which he took his title, and thereafter created in black and white fantasies which were a weird combination of woodcut style, of *pointillisme*, and of impressionistic light-effects. He had therefore to keep closely to Moussorgsky's score in the composition of his drawings, and to parcel out and divide his scenes in conformity with the music. Of course, in this case too the synchronism is very simple to carry out: for the artist has cut his film according to the music, and so the filming of the score by the sound-on-film process is all that remains to be done, and it is a problem more technical than artistic. The coincidence of length, rhythm, and dynamics was already established while the film itself was being made.

Yet another and very interesting construction is that of the film *Joie de Vivre*, drawn by Hoppin and Gross. In this case the Hungarian Tibor von Harsany composed the music, developing the original idea, in a fixed form, somewhat like a modified song form. The individual sections, formulated in the scheme ABC—Trio—CBA, are rhythmically rounded off to a hair. The work was done in co-operation with the draughtsmen: that is, after the composer had completed a section of his work, he played it to the artist and gave him the exact time-measurements as he did so. The calculation was simple enough: 24 pictures projected in a second. So if the composer wrote a bar in 4/4 time on the basis of a metronome ratio of 120 to a crotchet, one bar would last 2 seconds, that is, 48 film images. In this way, therefore, a draughtsman who knew nothing of music could, after examination of the score with its metronome data and number of bars, calculate exactly how to base the structure of his film, no matter what rhythm was concerned. He could also modify the rhythm according to the beat, so that, after the simultaneous completion of film and music, the synchronisation affords no problems at all. It is evident with what minute precision all sound-effects can be produced in these circumstances.

Musical quotation from the cartoon film *Joie de Vivre*. Music composed by Tibor von Harsany.

The sound-cartoon undoubtedly belongs to those forms of the musical film which not only now, but also in the future, will play a dominating part. In them the hyperdimensional tones produced by the 'handwritten sound-track' will probably find their first sphere of activity: but that subject will better be left for examination at the conclusion of this book.

Part Four: The Sound-Film

D. Forms and methods of composition

As in the silent film, so in the sound-film, most of the traditional musical forms are useless. Yet it is much easier to have single detached pieces of music in the sound-film than in the silent film. For the latter required a continuous illustration and formed a musical whole which, out of regard for the film, knew no distinctive features. But the sound-film has dramatically no continuous musical accompaniment, unless it be but a case of the resumption of silent-film technique with the sound-producing apparatus of the sound-film. On the contrary, it falls into single parts—dialogue scenes, song items, wordless portions, either with incidental noises or with music. Within these sections, as far as they can be treated musically, many opportunities for formal finish are given.

Of course, the days of compilation belong to· the past. To-day it is only a question of original compositions, and for this reason an artistic uniformity of style is more easily attainable than in those days.

We have already spoken of straightforward 'numbers'. Their most important effect in sound-films is derived from the preceding preparation made for them, as indicated above, in the section on sound-film operetta: the 'number' is developed from a rhythm and culminates in a climax which is identical with the number itself. So these single items must above all be rhythmically defined. Of course producers, needing their song hit, see to it that they also have effective melody. These claims do not always square with the musician's artistic sense; for him, the essential thing will always be that rhythm, atmosphere, and characteristics of the piece coincide with the corresponding scenes in the film. As an example of a number of this kind which successfully meets all requirements made of it we may here quote the theme-song of *Sous les toits de Paris* (by Moretti). Auric's score for *A nous la liberté* or Parys' music with *Le million* were also models of rhythmical preparation and constant line displayed from the first bars of the song to its conclusion. In Friedrich Holländer's composition accompanying the film *Einbrecher*, this gifted musician was one of the first to mix dumb show and film music with *buffo* elements; and the most important passages in a film that pictorially was fairly insignificant were exemplary

155

for the way in which they displayed the musical development of the film's plot to advantage, by means of a given rhythm (which was expressed in gestures, noises, or accented words).

As far as the wordless and songless passages are concerned, it would not be advisable, in view of the diversity of the sound-film form, for the music to be confined to pure illustration. It should be kept more strictly than before to self-chosen or self-created forms; it should avoid boundless descriptive passages of the old silent-film variety; and should assume an expressionistic rather than an impressionistic character. (These words are used in the sense defined above, Part Two, Section G, p. 74.) It has little time in which to develop, and therefore each single bar must have its logical justification. In the sound-film, the music can say much more than in the silent film: that is the big chance offered it by technical progress. It should therefore penetrate to the depths of the plot which it accompanies. To give a concrete example. In the film *Kuhle-Wampe*, there is a scene depicting a horde of cyclists running a race to win a position which will liberate them from the throes of unemployment: it would be in bad taste to write some allegro, in the style of former *Kinothek*, for this passage. No, one should indicate, as Hanns Eisler has indeed done, besides the tempo of the scene, the expression of embitterment and despondency among those cyclists. As moreover the scene formed a detached whole, a formal musical finish was also possible; the composer managed, without any risk of distracting the audience, to write a movement in fugal style which did honour to his artistry and hit off the characteristic mood of that particular section of the film. The whole piece was in the form of a symphonic scherzo, and could straightway be performed in the concert hall without losing any of its effect.

These two forms, the musical number based on rhythm, with its preparatory stages, and the detached item for a wordless scene (to-day naturalistic noises are dropping out more and more), are so far the two main kinds of musical forms in sound-films. They can of course be carried out in many variations. A traditional musical form which might be taken over for the sound-film is the 'Theme with variations'. This old musicians' ideal, in free treatment, presents the film with extraordinary possibilities. Again, some piece of music composed in an established form could be taken over bodily, in which case the film would later have to be fitted to it by means of the necessary cutting. The director, Fedor Ozep, in co-operation with the composer Karol Rathaus, often worked in this way with his films; readers may recollect the extremely successful scenes in his *Karamazov* film or in *Amok*, to take only two examples that prove how vital a constructive and significant agreement between film and music can be; they prove, further, that a film has nothing to lose, on the contrary it actually gains, by conforming to a well-built musical form.

But it must be borne in mind that generally the composer finds it hardly possible to preserve a compact form, because directors very often begin to make alterations on the film after the visuals and the music are finished. In this event, the composer is completely at the mercy of the editor's scissors and compelled, unless he is prepared to begin all his work from the beginning again, to look on while the normal organic growth that was his score is mutilated by cuts that are musically without sense at all: which happens more often than is commonly known. In films with musically important sections the composer should therefore have a free hand assured him by contract, to prepare his composition first within a certain limit of time, on which basis the editor can proceed to do his work. Only then is an agreement between rhythm and form possible.

As regards their procedure, composers, if they wish to work with systematic precision, will arrange their job as follows:

After the final cutting of the film, they will have it shown to them several times, so that a really exact picture of its structure and its dramatic climaxes is

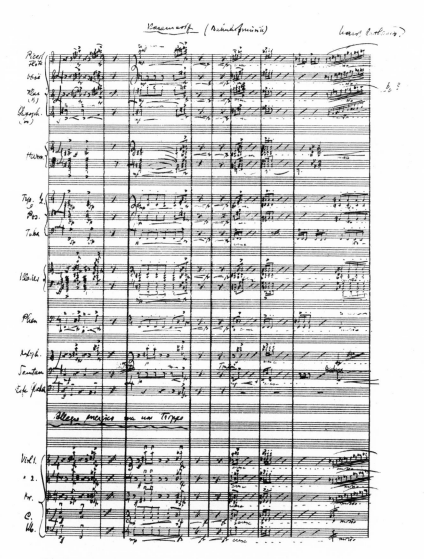

Railway-station music by Karol Rathaus for Ozep's *Karamazov* film. Facsimile of a page from the original score.

impressed on their brain. They will from the outset reflect on the points which are most important for the composition, to determine its form and character. Then they will dictate to a secretary, who is present during the course of a fresh performance, the contents of the manuscript in its musical aspects, that is, of course, only the scenes which will have to be set to music. In this way, they write a new scenario, with all the details required for composition. After this work is done, the individual sections are then measured with a stop-watch, so that their duration is firmly established. The outline of the composition can then begin.

Once that too is finished, the film is performed again, and the composer will on the basis of this outline be able to 'confront' the music with the film, which he will best be able to do by conducting it through for himself while the film is turned before him. Usually several mistakes are discovered in this process, which can at once be corrected. It must be noted that this work can only take place after the final cut or version of the film has been decided, although experience has shown that this does not prevent subsequent alterations from being made, to the detriment of the music!

The music, being composed and corrected, is now orchestrated and rehearsed. Before the sound-rehearsals at the microphone, very meticulous instrumental rehearsals are advisable, in order that the members of the orchestra may gain a complete technical command of the score. In the microphone rehearsals only a few cases of tone-retouching are permissible, because time is costly in the recording-rooms. But even at this stage the composer is often enough faced with the necessity for some alteration, which then involves especial skill and command of his art.

The musical recording of sound-films will in the future undoubtedly take place before or after the actual film-photography: on this point, for once—and it is an exception—musical and commercial considerations agree. For film composers this development is very favourable, as it gives them a field for their talents, in which they are only handicapped by the time-limits which are set them. For the future all those pretexts, with which bad musicians used once to excuse themselves, without possibility of anyone contradicting them with a good conscience, are abolished.

Eric Sarnette, in a chapter of his work on *Music and the Microphone* which is devoted to film music, writes with complete justification about a kind of film music which is supposed to belong to the past, but again and again, even in sound-films, returns to life: 'When the picture of an irate man appears, brass trumpets are heard; chubby-faced bassoons,

160

when a fat man is seen coming along; oboes, when a quiet valley with cattle is shown on the screen; plaintive violins to accompany a picture of a pair of lovers, more like a sentimental postcard than anything else. . . .'

These examples given by Sarnette could be multiplied a hundred times: a glance at the index of a compilation library is sufficient. But to-day this kind of thing is no longer good enough. For the days are over, once for all, when it could be said that the public took no account of film music. The visitor to a sound-film can and must take musical impressions away with him after the performance as well; and these are conscious—as opposed to those of the silent-film period. Whereas in the silent film everything was dependent on the eye, the ear is in the sound-film participant to a high degree in the perception of artistic pleasure. Eye and ear share the impression, each according to the significance of film and sound, and achieve an optical and acoustical synthesis which could never in the silent-film period have been attained, owing to the quite different and altogether subordinate part played by the illustrative music then in use.

Whereas at that time the two-dimensional film image and the plastic vitality of the music formed an alliance impossible in itself, now the two-dimensional image is wedded to music which is also on the plane, because it is transmitted by the same apparatus. The artistic, technical, and psychological 'blood groups', if we may use the term in this connection, coincide. All the conditions for the creation of a work of art, complete in every aspect, are thus given.

Technical contact changes the style of music, just as material influences, above all in the films, have already changed it in various respects. The film composer of the future will, with his all but inexhaustible technical means of expression, be able to allow his imagination the fullest scope, by virtue of mixing, cutting, and sound-manipulation of every kind. But he will not be in a position to develop that personal style which great masters of music have always had. In spite of the presupposed originality of his manuscript, he will for better or for worse be forced to bow to realities. A Proteus in modern guise, he will have to know how to do everything, to command every style, to adapt himself in spite of every kind of complication to the musical form demanded of him in each particular case and, in short, be possessed of an enormous mental mobility.

Gone is the romanticism which hovered over the musician of the nineteenth century. In the figure of the film composer we can also see the type of the future artist. The development of film music affords us a prophetic picture of times to come with their radical revaluation of all values. . . .

E. Orchestration problems of the Sound-film

Orchestra and instrumentation

Whave seen to what fundamental changes musical forms have been subjected by the sound-film. The instrumental frame in which they are interpreted has been still more the victim of a basic revolution, and differs in most material respects from traditional symphonic orchestration. The reason?—Between musicians and public there now stands the *microphone* as the dominating medium. Not for psychological reasons alone must a new trail be blazed: the laws of electrical science, or simply of physics itself, require co-operation between musicians and engineers, without whose researches and their results they would remain powerless in front of the microphone.

A new aesthetics of sound is coming into existence. To-day it is still in an embryonic stage, and is slowly growing as a result of experiment. We cannot yet establish a final scheme or theory of instrumentation for the microphone, because the details of sound-effects in the various recording systems are different, and because the conditions of sound-recording are hardly ever the same; furthermore, because the three microphonic arts, sound-films, wireless, and gramophone, are very similar, but nevertheless have different laws to which they are subject; and finally, because really systematic experiments have not yet been possible. The views of microphone composers on the capacities and application of individual instruments are not in agreement at all.

An attempt is made here to outline some fundamental principles, but the possibilities of the microphone's development must all the while be taken into account, for they are just as incalculable as its moods. For the microphone *has* moods; it displays preference and disinclination, has its favourites and its foes; to the annoyance of artists and technicians, it remains to-day as unreliable as ever. Its mechanism depends not only on the material used and the treatment accorded to it, but also on the atmospheric and acoustical conditions of the room in which it is set up, on the positioning of the instruments, the structure of the score, and a host of contingencies of every kind.

There is in addition a series of *imponderabilia* to be considered, which can change the original sound from the time of its production in the studio to its final effect on the spectator in the cinema. *Mutilation of tone* results during about five stages of a process in which, even with the most advanced technical devices, the exact original tone cannot possibly be preserved in its true state:

(1) the sound is photographed;

(2) it is printed from the negative on to the positive;

(3) then the mixing follows—the printing of other additional sound-strips with other music, speech, or noises on to the original sound-positive: here one has to reckon with the noises of three spools on the re-recording and mixing machines, however perfectly they function;

(4) the result is then printed on a synchronised copy (with the pictures belonging to it);

(5) the sound-picture strip which is thus made runs through the projection unit and reaches, after amplification, its final goal, the loudspeaker.

With so many intermediate stages, it is a miracle that transmissions sound as well as they generally do to-day. Contrasting the genesis of sound in gramophone recording, or in the still more direct process of broadcasting, we can readily recognise the much

165

greater difficulties attending the orchestration and the choice of instruments for sound-films.

The bow-instruments

When the motor was invented, says Sarnette, people did not at once build cars which answered the altered requirements of speed, but at first remained content with the old high form of carriage. It is the same with the microphone and the orchestra: the traditional symphony orchestra corresponds to the old type of carriage, according to Sarnette, and has to give way to the new microphone orchestra, with its special instruments created by the microphone, but not yet introduced into general use.

Musicians, it must be admitted, have not yet reached any great measure of agreement on this question. Sarnette's axiom that the stringed instruments should be taken out of the microphone orchestra has so far been supported by only a small group of composers. Hanns Eisler is generally regarded as their leader. Almost all the others, and not the worst among them, insist that the body of string-players is no less indispensable for the microphone than otherwise. Now the position was that something had to be done with the instrumental means which were in existence; one could not wait until new microphone instruments had been constructed and brought on the market. But, in spite of this practical consideration, the fact must be realised that the bow-instruments, for centuries the foundation of the orchestra, actually do *not* comply with the peculiar demands of the microphone.

In judging this question, we may perhaps start for once from a different point of view. Does it matter that the tone of an instrument such as the *violin* is transformed through the medium of the microphone into other than its accustomed sound-values? The process of production described above undoubtedly distorts the tone of the violin especially, and the microphone altogether neutralises the highly characteristic timbre of the violin. Violin-sounds, especially in combination with other instruments, are scarcely recognisable. We have to accept this fact, just as we have long ago accepted the fact of films in monochrome only. But once we have reached this point in our train of thought, then we can ask ourselves whether we could not dispense entirely with the violin, even with its changed tonality. To-day we must still reply in the negative: for its technical agility, its fire, its *finesses*, have been hitherto beyond the power of even the most perfect microphone instrument to replace. This does not mean that it will remain indispensable in the future as well: the microphone orchestra is on the threshold of decisive and revolutionary changes, to which the violin will

167

presumably fall a prey, because its range of colour receives too little shading in the course of loudspeaker reproduction. The microphone without doubt robs it of the vivid expression which is in itself its true possession, and changes it into an impersonal instrument. Its timbre can be varied but little by the number of violins employed; its own peculiar wealth of shading is completely cut off by the microphone. Artificial damping sounds badly, and its use must be discouraged. Experienced gramophone conductors only allow muted passages to be played in the piano part, without using the dampers. *Pizzicatos* are easily possible.

Opinions are extremely varied as to the number of bow-instruments, especially violins, to be employed for the sound-film microphone. Whereas for gramophone recording large parts are preferred, to achieve a full and round tone, the normal number of strings for a sound-film is mostly limited (even when the wind is of considerable strength) to 4 first and 4 second violins, 3 violas, 2 violoncellos, and 1 double-bass. The employment of a big orchestra of string-players, as used by Paul Dessau for the music of his Fanck films, remains an exception; although in concert films a large body of strings is necessitated by the pictures of the orchestra in action.

Sound-distortions of *violas* and *'cellos* are not so violent as in the case of violins; like most instruments of the middle range, they sound agreeably in reproduction, even though they too are not immune from a certain change in tone. The *double-basses*, on the other hand, have long given the musical directors knotty problems to solve: their *pizzicato* was almost impossible, and their *forte*, on account of the vibrations of their long and thick strings, no less so. In this case, technical progress has adapted itself to the instrument. By careful positioning on the set, by avoidance of *sforzandos* and *pizzicatos*, a solution of the difficulties was gradually brought nearer: not indeed by overcoming them, but by going out of their way. The double-bass will probably, next to the violin, be the bow-instrument most likely to be eliminated at an early stage from the microphone orchestra, in so far as special effects do not justify its inclusion. It is not 'microgenic'!

The sound-film microphone undoubtedly requires a big reduction in the quantity of instruments employed. If the differences in opinion on the use of the strings are to be resolved in a (for the time being) positive form, then *transparency of tone*, and its effect of a chamber orchestra, must be achieved by a diminution of the bow-instruments, approximately in the numerical ratio given above. This is equally valid for the co-operation of the strings in a big orchestra; these parts would otherwise appear thick and pulpy through linear distortions.

The need or otherwise of strings in a sound-film

169

orchestra is decided finally, apart from all technical considerations, according to the plot and style of the film which has to be set to music. A microphone orchestra without strings would for instance be unsuitable for an average society film or for an old-fashioned sound-film operetta. Thus the tyranny of the microphone is not the only determining factor in the constitution of the orchestra for each film, but—wisely enough—the film as well, with its choice of plot and scheme of production. For this reason alone the greater part of the conflict around the violins in sound-film orchestras is to-day still superfluous. Only when the sound-film itself leaves its well-worn ruts, to enter on its own and true proper domain, will a solution of the microphone-instrument problem become absolutely necessary.

The wind instruments

(*a*) *Wood-wind.* Their specific suitability for the microphone is proven and irrefutable. Almost all the instruments in the wood-wind family come through faultlessly in loudspeaker reproduction.

Flutes have if anything still a few dangerous notes. The lower register of the bass flute occasionally distorts; more dangerous are the high notes of the piccolo, which is best avoided on account of its high frequencies. The frequency range of the equipment in general use has its higher and lower limits; beyond them, overtones are cut off, in the case of deep-pitched instruments the fundamentals, with the result that the original tone is reproduced in an altered or distorted form.

The *oboe* and *cor anglais* come through perfectly. Their highest notes are not to be recommended at any time, and still less for the sound-film microphone. The use of these instruments for the microphone remains a matter of taste. Many modern composers, who have removed the strings from their orchestras or reduced their number, do not employ them, because their all too characteristic timbre disturbs, in their view, the harmonic unity of the orchestra.

The whole *clarinet* family furnishes ideal microphone instruments. To them belong also *saxophones*. Here there are no dangers of any kind in recording.

Bassoons can likewise be used to advantage. Their dry, subdued note is pre-eminently suited for mechanical reproduction.

(b) *Brass.* *Horns* are as much a matter of dispute as violins. The majority of composers no longer use them for sound-films, whilst others assert that they have had good experience with them. They caused many technical difficulties in recording in the early days of the sound-film, until the horn-players had learnt not to take the note so sharply and fully as

171

usual, but to blow at lower pressure. The horn is in itself easily dispensed with in the microphonic orchestra; its functions could be well, indeed better, undertaken by the alto saxophone, for instance. The danger of 'bubbling' is moreover one which the best of horn-players cannot avoid sometimes: in this event, the whole record, however good it otherwise be, must be repeated once more. In addition, the horn suits the style of very few films indeed.

By sound-mixtures, which are inspired by the microphone, not only can novel harmonic combinations be created, but existing harmonic characters can be reconstructed. The horn, for example, can be reproduced in microphone technique by a unison of a trumpet in low range and a trombone in high range. Such a combination will exclude the specific dangers attendant upon the use of the horn.

Trumpets come up excellently, though they lose their brilliant tone in mechanical reproduction.

Trombones of every register sound very well, and can be used, like trumpets, without danger, either with or without muting.

All kinds of *tubas*, which occur relatively seldom, have a faultless intonation; sousaphones are hardly used any more, except perhaps in jazz bands.

Stringed instruments, hammered or plucked

The *harp* possesses an excellent, sometimes almost too good, tone. Its lower notes must be given with the greatest caution, as otherwise they penetrate too violently. The higher and middle ranges are the best. Equally good is the *banjo*. *Lute, mandoline, guitar*, and *harpsichord* can be employed without danger, save that care must be taken not to obscure them with other instruments.

The *pianoforte*—in the beginning of sound-films a special source of anxiety to sound-directors—under present-day conditions of recording generally sounds well. An essential factor is absolute purity of pitch. But a warning must be given against the recording of piano solo passages. The piano is best used in the microphonic orchestra as a supplementary instrument; its bass notes are especially convenient to round off the harmonics of other instruments, above all in distinctly rhythmic passages. The piano in the microphonic orchestra takes the part rather of an instrument to accentuate the rhythm, and is very useful as such.

Special instruments

The *xylophone* belongs to the best class of microgenic instruments. In all its ranges, it can be used equally well. The *celesta* can also sound effective: its delicate tone enjoys an excellent reproduction.

The *accordion*, an instrument used very much in France, is technically not dangerous in transmission, but its effect quickly palls. The *vibraphone* should be used with caution and only seldom, because its strong vibrations only have their full value at the end of a piece of music, otherwise only creating an unintended connection with the following bars.

Harmonium and *organ* are in general, owing to their rounded sound-production, heard to advantage through the microphone, provided that, especially in the case of the organ pedals and in strong accentuation of the dynamics, they do not produce too many violent sound-waves. Thus their use in *fortissimo* should be limited; the best intonation would be given by high and middle notes from a bare *forte* to the softest *pianissimo*. In addition, they are useful with other instruments in producing new harmonic combinations. Nevertheless care should be taken in using them that their tone does not handicap the transparency of the orchestra, because they can very easily blur the clarity of the instrumentation.

Percussion

The instruments under this category are some of the most problematical, from the point of view of microphone technique. Whereas the overtones of the violins are cut off and so distort the sound, the fundamentals of the biggest percussion instruments are still

174

absent. The sound-frequency range of the apparatus has its higher limit, on the average 10,000 cycles, and its lower, at 100 cycles. The notes of percussion instruments have their fundamentals so deadened that they turn to dryness without any resonance.

The *kettledrum*, for instance, is one of the most difficult instruments to record to-day. If it is struck too softly, its note does not penetrate; if it is too loud, its tone 'booms' in a most unpleasant way. In this case, experiments have to be made for every one of the recording systems, in which an essential factor will be the relative position of the instrument and the microphone.

Experiences with the *bass drum* vary. It is almost as difficult to record as the kettledrum, but the results obtained with it have not been quite so bad. It is occasionally used as a substitute for the kettledrum, because its timbre gives a livelier reproduction. As far as the *side drum* is concerned, it is among those percussion instruments which are relatively simple for the sound-camera to subdue. Selmar Meyrowitz even tried the experiment, during gramophone recording, of placing side drums near the microphone, and so gained a great effect. When struck with a certain amount of care and used discreetly in the score, the side drum boasts quite a few interesting possibilities in effect, which can be employed with comparatively little danger.

175

Of the other percussion instruments, *glockenspiels* record very well, in every variety down to the Javanese *gamelans*, the effect of which (several original shots in cultural films may recur to memory) is very striking. *Gongs* (*tam-tams*), and *tom-toms*, used with caution, are of great effect, all the more if they only occur in brief passages here and there; the *triangle* affords no difficulty, whereas the *cymbals* (in contrast with the excellent reproduction of the *tambourine*) should only be used with extreme care, especially as they lose the penetrative quality of their note in the loudspeaker.

An important factor with all percussion is the quality of the recording system. In high-fidelity apparatuses, which have been able to extend their frequency range considerably in both directions, far less difficulties are encountered: the RCA or the new Western Electric units occur to mind.

What effects can with skilful orchestral treatment be got from percussion, is shown by a passage in the score of *Amok*. Here Karol Rathaus used 3 kettledrums, a xylophone, 3 tom-toms, a Chinese tam-tam, 3 gongs, a low-pitched glockenspiel, a vibraphone, bass drum and side drum, and cymbals. When reproduced, this mighty noise-mechanism makes a great impression that is hardly impaired at all by distortion.

Funeral music by Karol Rathaus for Ozep's *Amok*.
Please note the simultaneous use of thirteen percussion instruments!

Electrical instruments

These are not to be regarded as primarily micro-phonic instruments, although some of them un-doubtedly have capacity for good tone-reproduction. As they themselves develop their tone indirectly, that is, through a loudspeaker, one must reckon with mutilation of sound as a result of the duplication of the intermediate electrical stages. Nevertheless, a few of them enrich the microphone orchestra with tone-colours hitherto unheard of. Before all others, let us recommend the *Ondium Martenot*, the appar-atus derived from Theremin's ether-wave music, but with the sound-scale anchored on a keyboard, so that no sound-fluctuations are possible (as with There-min's apparatus) which would be intolerable in the microphone.

This kind of electrical instrument, of which there are already quite a number of similar types, can only be played in a single part, but then they are possessed of a full range of tone-modulations. With skilful in-strumentation they can be used as substitutes for several instruments of different kinds. Their intona-tion, which has unheard-of dynamic reserves, re-tains its quality very well in reproduction. There is no doubt that in the microphonic orchestra of the future 'ether-wave music' will be used: indeed, it is already a regular feature in Arthur Honegger's film scores. An interesting example of its use is given by Shostakovitch in the Russian film *Shame* (*Counter-plan*): there it is not only music, but also noise-apparatus. In a French film by Jean Lods, *Le Mil*, which has as its plot the physical training of an athlete, the interesting experiment is made of giving the accompaniment solo to the Ondium Martenot. This, however, is an effect which should be reserved for exceptional cases.

The Bechstein-Nernst grand piano, erected by the great scholar Nernst with the assistance of the Siemens Company, is not bad microphonically, but is, after all, a substitute for celesta, *harpsichord* (which can be reproduced extremely well), and harmonium. In consequence, its presence in the microphonic orchestra would appear to be necessary more on economic than on artistic grounds. Certain doubts would indeed not be out of place, as its tone too passes through a loudspeaker. Only those electrical instruments should be incorporated with the microphonic orchestra which, like the Ondium Martenot, really produce quite new sounds. The others may be left to serve living music for experimental purposes. In this category may be classed electrical stringed instruments, the Jörg Mager organ, and all attempts that have been made with the piano. The Trautonium (developed in the Berlin State Academy of Music), one of the first electrical instru-

178

ments of interest, for which Hindemith among others has written compositions, was entirely superseded by the Ondium type, and in any case would hardly have been a candidate for reproduction owing to the uncertainty of its intonation.

With the exception of those electrical instruments which produce a basically new sound, we stand on principle for direct playing before the microphone, in so far as musicians have still to attend to instruments at all. There are enough physical and chemical processes intervening, before the sound of performing artists is emitted from the loudspeaker; unless it is absolutely necessary, the distance between players and listeners should not be extended still farther.

The human voice

This outlined theory of instrumentation for microphonic purposes must end with the voice as the most important factor of all, for human actors dominate the sound-film. The human throat is the principal microphonic instrument. In this case, the problem is not only one of beauty of tone in itself, but also of clear and immaculate word-phrasing. It is even more essential in sound-films than in opera that every single word sung and spoken must be intelligible, if the film is not to be regarded as a failure.

The sound-film has created a completely new style

of phrasing and accentuation of word-syllables in song. It must be emphasised that a primitive device like the muffling of the orchestra is not enough. We are concerned with a new technique of singing, which produces a unity of word and tone by adaptation of the music to the phrase. Kurt Weill in his song works showed the way, and it should be followed by the sound-film and its composers.

The sharp pronunciation of final consonants, until a short time ago, and especially in the early days of sound-films, one of the greatest problems, is to-day made possible by the improvements in the recording apparatus. Since modern units can in extreme cases respond to frequencies up to 15,000 cycles—high sibilant notes are, as is well known, of especially high frequency—the rightly phrased and well-sung word can be recorded with great distinctness.

The air-supply, that is, breathing in and out, is likewise based on special laws: the best way is to breathe in through the mouth and out through the nose. The voices best suited to the microphone are thin, nasal, closed voices. Big, broad, shrill, or even tremulous organs not only lose all their effect in the loudspeaker, but suffer considerable distortion and sound badly. A new phonetic theory of song for microphonic needs is in course of development together with the new theory of instrumentation for microphonic orchestras.

Choirs are, and for the present will continue to be, unsuitable for the sound-film. The capacity of the recording units is not yet adequate to register the plastic character of a multitude of voices; but, just as the choir in 'living' performances can very seldom be understood word for word, so it cannot reckon on being understood by anyone at all through the loud-speaker. And since one of the conditions for the success of a sound-film is that the words should be correctly understood, the choir can only be used as a means of dynamic expression, or at best to convey colour or atmosphere. On no account is polyphony to be recommended. A simple diction, preferably with one or two voice-parts, is best.

Individual languages are by no means equally good instruments for microphone reproduction. Some are easier to record than others. The easiest is always Italian, followed by English, then come French and Spanish, and finally German and Russian, with their many pointed consonants and gutturals.

General problems of orchestration

For the body of instrumental and vocal music in sound-films, a few hitherto generally valid principles hold good.

There is neither a genuine pianissimo nor a good fortissimo. If the sound-recordist muffles his potentiometer, he does not thereby obtain a *pp* in the sense

181

interpreted in living music, but merely a weakening in the volume of a sound that originally was stronger in amplification; and at the opposite extreme, in *ff* playing, there still occur, even in the most perfect reproduction, those linear distortions which weaken and mutilate the mighty and brilliant and broad intonation of reality. So the film composer must reckon with this factor and control his dynamics accordingly, by his phrasing, instrumentation, and contrast-effects. Herein we see one of the most fundamental differences between living music and that which is mechanically reproduced. Technique, however far advanced it be, has still not yet reached a level which would admit of a score being recorded absolutely true to note. Since this expectation is illogical, because music has to conform with the prevalent technical conditions, it follows that a revolutionary change-over to the situation required by the available apparatus will have to take place. So the instrumentation of the sound-film orchestra is governed by rules which are essentially different from those governing the symphony orchestra.

This change of attitude had best begin in the very conception of the music. There is no point in overloading it with excessively rich chords, just as it is not advisable to exaggerate the number of parts in the music. To indicate plainly what is required, one could maintain that a good movement in two mel-

odic parts is best suited to the sound-film, provided
those parts do not lie too close to one another. This
principle, which is carried out often enough in practice, sheds an illuminating light on the requirements
of film-musical structure: clarity of line and transparency of tone.

From these principles the conclusion follows that
ripieno (parts used to fill in) should very seldom be
left in the score. They must in general be avoided,
because they impair the plastic character of the tone.
Duplications should likewise be omitted as much as
possible, except where definite instrumental combinations, that is, intentional sound-effects, are sought.

Apart from the aesthetic considerations prompting
these general rules, there are also technical and physical grounds for them. A fully constituted orchestra
with *ripieno* and duplicated parts, playing moreover
in a *forte*, in loudspeaker reproduction almost invariably results in a complete chaos of sound, in which
the plastic nature of the tone is entirely lost and un-
differentiated harmonies in distorted form are alone
audible. This is owing to the so-called combination
tones, called Tartini's tones after their discoverer,
the famous violin virtuoso. They always occur when-
ever in any part of the reproduction unit the effect is
not proportional to the effectual power. If the original tone already consists of a series of different
tones (as in an orchestral piece) with numerous over-

tones, a multitude of combination tones are formed in addition, which turn the original harmony into an unpleasant dissonance. For this reason alone it follows as a practical necessity that the microphone orchestra should be constituted on a small scale: for it is not the quantity of executants that determines the quality of tone, but rather the way in which the instrumental groups are combined. For sound-film effect, an ensemble consisting of five players can theoretically match one of fifty players, if it does not actually surpass it.

We know of two alternatives for instrumental sound-colouring in sound-film accompaniment: the one derived from the symphony orchestra, with its self-imposed limitations, and adapting itself as well as possible to the particular requirements of the microphone; the other, blazing the trail into unknown country, with a wind orchestra without strings, and abandoning the traditional kinds of symphonic instrumentation, as radically as a jazz orchestra shuns the form of old-fashioned chamber orchestras.

An example of microphonic instrumentation in an orchestra of the traditional type is given in the accompanying bars from the Machaty film *Ecstasy*, by Giuseppe Becce (see musical facsimile). Above an harmonic tremolo movement there is a melody for a single clarinet, supplemented by a bassoon and a horn. The harp adds a few high-lights. That is all;

184

Facsimile from the original score of the music composed by Giuseppe Becce for Gustav Machaty's Czech film *Ecstasy*.

but it indicates in exemplary manner the only possible combination of traditional orchestral style with consideration for the exigencies of microphone technique. The transparent character of the orchestra allows the microphone a plastic recording.

A contrast which is almost droll now follows: it is the railway-station music for Ozep's fine *Karamazov* film, composed by Karol Rathaus (see musical facsimile). Here a full orchestra is used, in the perfect style of symphonic concerto; yet this music was one of the earliest film compositions of real worth, and was moreover the first which Rathaus wrote for the films. But such *tutti* passages have become very rare indeed—or at least they should attain the status of rarities! They have their justification in the bars here quoted, and occasionally scenes will occur, in which for better or for worse the composer will have to entrust his work to the good or bad humour of the recording apparatus. But in general a specialised type of instrumentation for the microphone should be able to achieve dynamic effects without the employment of traditional *tuttis*.

The instrumental structure of an orchestra for wind alone has naturally a quite different appearance. In a typical instance of an orchestral movement by Eisler (see musical facsimile), piano, banjo and percussion give the rhythmical and harmonic foundations. The wind is used for the solo parts; to this

185

orchestra belong clarinets, saxophones, trumpets, and trombones, but neither flutes nor oboes. The tone thus becomes more austere and more neutral; the polyphony is heard with inexorable clarity. The microphone reproduces these sound-combinations with greater pliancy and sets the melodic lines in much bolder relief against one another than if they were mixed with the tones of stringed instruments. In view of the risk of their being distorted, the ensemble is more microgenic without them.

We do not overlook the perils attendant on such a microphonic orchestral technique; they would seem to be centred in a certain systematisation of tone. But Eisler has shown in the course of his film-musical activity how far an elimination of the strings from sound-film orchestras is possible. We shall, in our treatment of the problem of actual microphone instruments, see that the apostles of the wind orchestra for sound-films actually fall into line with those who maintain the basic diversity of music recorded through the microphone and transmitted through the loudspeaker, and wish to unfetter it from every tradition—not only in respect of instrumentation, but also of content and form.

Seating of the microphone orchestra

As well as the instrumentation, another decisive factor in recording is the positioning of the players in relation to the microphone and to the acoustics of the set. Paul Dessau suggests an ideal kind of seating, admittedly very expensive to carry out: each musician is seated on a movable chair, which can be driven at the conductor's will, by means of electrical driving gear, nearer to or farther from the microphone, according to the indications of the score and the sound-recordist. Without a doubt, this would do away with the rigid positioning hitherto inevitable: for the players can hardly indulge in a constant coming and going during the performance, and movable microphones are not always satisfactory.

There is no one ideal arrangement of the orchestra in front of the microphone. Hitherto a general scheme has been followed: the percussion and double-basses farthest away from the instrument, then in progressive stages further forward piano, brass, wood-wind, and strings. Solos are usually played close in front of or next to the microphone. The tone can be varied by setting up more than one microphone. The sound-recordist as he listens will in each particular case decide on a slightly altered positioning of the orchestra or of the microphone, judging by the characteristics of the score. Of course, if this sound-recordist is no musician, or is not possessed at least of an extremely fine ear and sense of the balance of orchestral tone (and unfortunately he very rarely has this gift), then he will with difficulty be able to reach agreement

187

with the conductor, should the latter once listen to the music from the recording box. The quality of the tone stands or falls by the work of the sound-recordist. It is hard to understand why film companies have not long ago instituted schools for sound-recordists, just as there are schools for projector operators. No sound-recordist ought to superintend and decide on the sound-structure of a sound-film without having received a thorough musical and technical training.

So we can see that the problem of the instrumentation of a piece of sound-film music is by no means ended with the writing of the score: even during the performance before the microphone a whole series of modifications may possibly be required, which goes to show that one cannot bend the microphone to one's will, but on the contrary must bow to its caprices. This recognition, above all, was the beginning of an entirely new technique of instrument construction, and the justification of the theory adduced that the microphone must have its own instruments to be able to reproduce a sound-vision in precise contours.

Microphone instruments

Every country has its specialities: Italy produced the finest violins, France has from the first been the home of the finest wind-instruments. Richard

Wagner had his *Ring* instruments built by the great
Adolphe Sax in Paris, and he knew very well what
he was doing. So we cannot wonder that the earliest
experiments in the construction of microphone instruments took place in Paris. There Eric Sarnette
(who has the dual advantage of being at the same
time both composer and sound-engineer), together
with Adolphe Sax junior, elaborated a number of
microphone instruments, some of which have already been officially introduced as such in the United
States.

We mean here by microphone instruments those
constructed with a view to the special requirements
of the microphone. It follows as a necessary corollary
that such a new instrument must be so made that it
can—from a commercial standpoint—be put to general use.

The nucleus of the problem in the work of Sarnette and Sax lay in finding out why it is that individual instruments in certain keys have a good effect
when heard directly by the ear, but in microphone
recording and loudspeaker reproduction are subject
to tonal changes. Furthermore, it had been ascer-
tained of certain instruments that different registers
were recorded through the microphone in unequal
quality. Two small examples: it was discovered that
the tuba in C is better suited for the microphone,
while that in B♭ sounds better to the human ear;

again, it was established that in the case of the B♭ trumpet only the B♭, D, E, and F tones sound equally well in the human and in the mechanical ear, whereas the other registers produce varied effects of unequal value.

Sarnette succeeded after lengthy experimental work in which he had a wind orchestra of fourteen artists at his disposal, in discovering a whole series of modifications in the construction of instruments, and partly in creating quite new types of instruments. In his book, *Music and the Microphone*, he describes the results of these experiments in broad outline.

New productions were a contra-bass clarinet, the saxhorn (a new form of tuba with a movable body or 'bell'), the alto clarinet made of metal, and the saxotromba (the old tuba, also with a fully adjustable bell). Among the instruments which were greatly modified, we may mention the sax-trombones with four mechanical pistons or valves; an alteration in the shape of the bell on the bass trumpet, which should play a greater part in the microphonic orchestra than it did in the symphony orchestra, as well as a change in the construction of the dampers to meet the special requirements of the microphone (see illustrations).

With the results of this creative technique of instrumental construction, a number of fresh possibilities have been presented and new paths to further research opened up. The value of these instruments will of course be proved above all at the microphone, but they possess besides a perfect mechanism and an excellent tone production for normal use. The saxhorns, for instance, in their new form, it is asserted, will no longer be limited to harmonic underlining alone, but thanks to their extreme mobility and their soft tone will also be carried for solo purposes. The performance of a quartet for saxhorns by Sarnette proved this to the hilt in Paris. The family of tubas thereby attained a sphere of influence hitherto denied them altogether.

The saxotromba solves in itself the problem of closeness to and distance from the microphone. Its bell is adjustable in such a way that its tone effects can be completely changed by moving it. That the sax-trombone with four valves likewise represents a considerable advancement in playing technique, is easily understood; its chief advantage lies in its facile execution and its purity. A new kind of trumpet possesses six valves; while the material of the B♭ clarinet is metal.

As regards the new shape of trumpet bell, which is intended as well for most of the brass instruments, it is based on the principle of preventing loss of sound, and yet of sacrificing nothing of the original tone of the instrument. Changes in the dampers were long due, even before the microphone came along with

191

its own needs; the old dampers not only muffled the sound, but distorted it as well. The new damper, above which a wire gate is fixed, aims at a diminution of sound-intensity and a weakening of its range of audibility, without however distorting it. Formerly the sound had been, so to speak, cut off, whereas with the new damper its vibrations can develop in spite of the damping.

For the microphone the solution of the problem of such a damper technique is most significant: it brings with it the advantages of moving the sound nearer or farther away, which with instruments like the trumpet cannot, as in the case of the saxo-tromba, be occasioned by adjustment of the bell. Besides that, the palette of tone-colours is greatly enriched thereby.

By virtue of these instrumental effects, Sarnette, the sound-engineer turned composer, could now preach a new aesthetics of instrumentation. He avoids the use of strings. His scores generally show the following instruments: clarinets, alto clarinets, contra-bass clarinets, bugles, trumpets, bass-trumpets, 3 sax-trombones, 4 saxhorns (see musical facsimile). With this orchestra experiments and recordings were made on various occasions, and these actually showed an amazing clarity and pliancy of sound. And forthwith Sarnette was in a position to establish certain principles of a new theory of instrumentation.

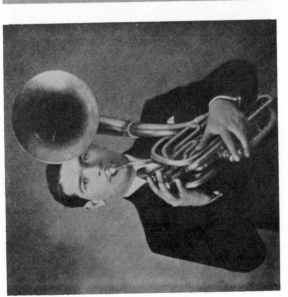

Saxhorn (Tuba) with adjustable 'bell'

Sax-trombones with mechanical valves

Bass-trumpet with the new microphone 'bell'

Sarnette's basic principle rests on an enlargement and extension of harmonies, in order to avoid overlapping of semitones. This principle corresponds to the demand we made above, that the melodic lines should not be drawn too close together. Enough free space should be left between the individual registers to allow the high, middle, and low melodic lines to stand in bold relief against one another.

He advocates instrumental combinations for one single melodic line (no duplications!), in order to evoke new microgenic sound-colours, such as—to quote only one instance—the unison of alto clarinet and bugle. In connection with this Sarnette demands a complete abandonment of the tonality of the normal symphony orchestra with string-players. According to him, one should not even imitate the sound of strings with wind-instruments. In other words, microphonic instrumentation requires a new kind of composition technique, of instrumental form and of musical feeling as a whole.

Sarnette goes so far in his aversion to strings, and especially to violins, as to doubt their worth even outside the framework of the microphonic orchestra, and to attribute their influence to a 'feminist' movement in music. That seems to us to be somewhat exaggerated, but on the other hand it is intelligible, because protagonists of new principles invariably fight for them in a spirit of intolerance for any other school of thought. In the normal symphony orchestra, the strings should still be as indispensable as they have proved to be for centuries, so long as the musical traditions of opera and concerts are continued in their present form—although even here there are already scores without strings or at least without violins (Stravinsky's *Symphony of Psalms*, Hindemith's concertos for wind, etc.). In the microphonic orchestra, on the other hand, when a reformation of the orchestral constituents and of film mentality does once take place, the strings will be the first instruments of the old tradition to be sacrificed to the new ideas.

Thus Sarnette's principles, wisely enough, not only concentrate on the use of modified wind-instruments, but also demand a clean and plastic method of composition. For his orchestra conceals nothing; the almost pitiless clarity of sound-production requires of composers that their every note should have sense and meaning. The days of romantic sound-painting with chords and sound-mixtures of indefinite nature are over. Schreker's opera, *Der ferne Klang*, gave way to a near and tangible ideal of tone belonging to our own time. For the serious musician, this is one of the most valuable of Sarnette's ideas.

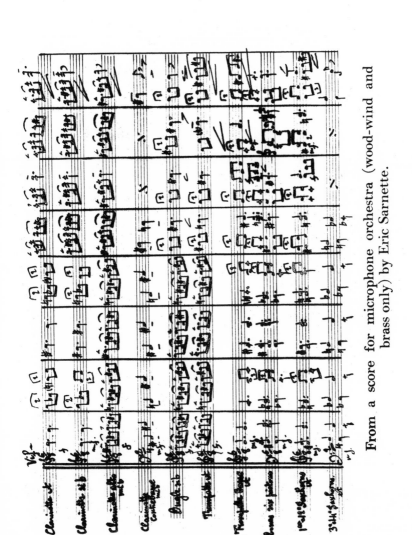

From a score for microphone orchestra (wood-wind and brass only) by Eric Sarnette.

Part Four: The Sound-Film

F. A forecast:
The handwritten sound-track

If we compare the opinions and experiences of experts on the subject of the sound-film microphone, we soon discover that there are very few points on which general agreement has yet been reached. One of these few is the suitability of wind-instruments for transmission, but a statement of the instruments preferred at once gives rise to differences of opinion. The question of the strings has hitherto remained the most disputed and the least elucidated.

That the requirements of the microphone are other than those of the opera-house or the concert-hall, is naturally no longer a matter of serious discussion, but the far-reaching change in musical aesthetics, as the very consequence of the microphone, seems as yet to be still considerably underestimated by most musicians. For it is not simply a question of whether the tone sounds well in reproduction. The point is

195

much more the transformation of the whole organism of microphone music—in our special case, of film music—to meet the requirements of the film and the microphone. Whether these experiments will be made in Eisler's way or in accordance with Sarnette's still more progressive claims—whether the attempt will actually one day be made to eliminate human performers altogether and to compose music on the basis of a sketch consisting of various patterns ('handwritten sound')—that is all a question of development, of experience, of films and the effects obtained.

We are admittedly not yet so rich in instrumental tonalities that we can afford, here and now, to throw whole groups of instruments right out of the orchestra. Arthur Honegger very rightly says that the real point is to enrich the sound-colour, and not to impoverish it. If new instruments appear which produce new timbres, then others can be eliminated which do less justice to the microphone orchestra.

But the musical progress of film music, we cannot emphasise this too often, depends not only on the achievements of the sound-technicians and composers, but also on the standard of the film industry. We are always in the same vicious circle: without the co-operation of producers, it will be impossible to obtain really profound innovations, or, to put it less strongly, the general development will be held up an

196

unduly long time by a strictly commercial attitude and an underestimation of the possibilities of educating their public.

The prospects of such progress are to-day quite impossible to forecast. What will it be like, if at some future date human interpreters can be altogether dispensed with in the recording of photographed music? if the sounds of the music transmitted through the loudspeaker gradually deviate more and more from the normal? and if the public accustoms itself to hear new sound-dimensions in the cinema, just as it has accustomed itself to take account of new picture-dimensions? Then conceivably one might, at least with a number of specialised films, do without an orchestra, and instruct a composer to put his music together in patterns on paper, which would then be photographed and produce a very strange and quite unreal sound.

This system of the 'handwritten sound-track', invented by Rudolf Pfenniger (and in a similar form by Oscar Fischinger), is based on the following physical hypotheses:

We know how sound-vibrations can be recorded on wax for gramophone reproduction, or on film for photographic reproduction. On a graph their image is equivalent to continually rising and falling wave-movements. Now these waves are produced photographically by a complicated system; but, the inven-

197

tors argued, one could draw them direct by hand, and win sound from non-existence. For to-day science is so far advanced that the lines of sound-pictures physically created can be calculated and copied. The oscillograph made it possible to ascertain the specific character of every single sound-track.

With pen and brush Pfenniger draws the desired sound-curves, has them photographed, and then is able to reproduce them on any normal sound-on-film system. This method cheapens the whole recording procedure by a full third of the total.

Theoretically, sounds of the most diverse kinds can now be represented graphically: natural sounds, organ-like tones, unknown instrumental timbres, choral effects. The sound-production of this hand-written sound-track in the first experiments—which, intelligibly enough, were made in connection with sound cartoons—gave the impression of a remarkable abstraction of tone, reminiscent of certain electrical instruments, which can be traced to the absence of overtones. Extremely effective are dynamic contrasts. Difficulties are presented by polyphony, which were evaded cleverly by extraordinarily rapid *arpeggios*. Two parts are generally used—which in no way conflicts with established principles.

Here we are started on a long road in quite unexplored country; a road which as yet runs beyond human control, leading to a magic realm created out of nothing. Instrumental and choral effects of unknown dimensions and singular tonality are presaged. Chance and the diversity of human states will be everywhere eliminated.

It is not impossible that the film of the future will seek to employ the handwritten sound-track for some of its music. And herein we may see further evidence of the future possibilities of film music, whose present-day condition is nothing but intensive preparation for the time when it will be able to free itself from the restraining influences of musical tradition, and attain its own individuality.

Part Four: The Sound-Film

3. The Problem of Acoustics in recording and reproduction
A. The creation of resonance and reverberation in recording

It is well known that in sound-recording for film or gramophone, despite excellent equipment, gifted composers, and well-trained technical staff, it is still difficult to obtain a plastic effect and satisfactory resonance in reproduction. It is also a known fact that these difficulties very often are due to the acoustical properties of the studio in which the recording is carried out. It is true that attempts have been made repeatedly in recent years to put modern scientific discoveries in acoustics to practical use: studios have been built with adjustable sound-sets, and microphones have been greatly improved. Many new elaborations have also taken place in the recording units of the sound-on-film system, as well as in the raw film stock. But the live quality of the sound is still missing, and the records sound flat and bloodless on the most costly reproducing apparatus.

200

The creation of resonance

Just as a man without healthy colouring looks ill, even so does the tone suffer, if it does not carry with it that resonance which is, as it were, its healthy complexion. It need not be a huge reverberation: in fact, that seems only very seldom applicable. But there is almost always a lack of diversity in reverberation, according to the studio or open-air set in which it has to appear.

Even apart from acoustical characteristics, it quite often happens that the processes of electro-acoustical recording take too little account of the fact that in musical recording it is not sufficient to provide the usual listening controls and, even where several microphones are installed, to regulate the sound on a single lead, without first of all dividing the sound into its three natural ranges: the upper, middle, and lower sections of the sound-system.

A great deal has been done towards a solution of this problem by the French musicians and sound-engineers, Sarnette (whom we already know for his microphone instruments), Camzon, and Sollima. They evolved in the Bernard Roux laboratory in Paris a new system of sound-recording which is striking in its logic and simplicity, and has the additional advantage, in practice, of installation at no great cost.

The basic principles of this system of 'electrical resonance, which can be regulated from the trans-

mitting station by means of divided sound-recording',
can be easily understood from the accompanying plan:

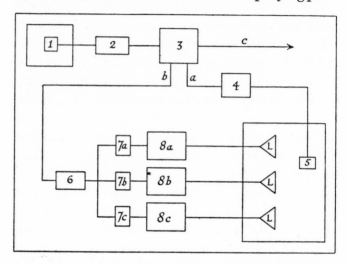

From the studio, which contains the recording microphone *1*, a wire passes over the pre-amplifier *2* to
the main amplifier *3*. From here three wires branch
off. Wire *a* runs via a pre-amplifier *4* to a further
microphone *5* in the so-called 'resonance chamber',
where the actual artificial production of resonance
takes place. Here the three loudspeakers *L* are set
up: the first for the higher, the second for the middle,
and the third for the lower sound-range. Wire *b* runs
to the adjustable control station *6*, and thus com-
mands the control panel for the three loudspeakers
in the resonance chamber. Each of the three loud-

speakers is provided with a regulable band pass filter *7a, b,* and *c,* and an amplifier *8 a, b,* and *c.*

Thus the sound-records proceeding from the studio do not simply pass over the usual amplifiers and single control stations to the recording unit, but are conducted in trebly regulated control to a further microphone in the resonance chamber, and only then do they travel on wire *c* to the recording apparatus.

The tone which is 'stereoscopically' treated in this process can further, by the mere turning of a knob, be given a changed effect, just as if it had been recorded in a small, a medium-sized, or a large studio. For the effects of the resonance chamber can likewise be adjusted as desired. The sound-recordist listening at the control station *6* can observe the conductor through a window, and also has the score in front of him. He has almost unlimited potentialities of sound light-and-shade and of reverberation adjustment at his disposal. He can avoid those dreaded linear distortions in orchestral *tuttis,* and flatness of tone, and he can also enliven the musical interpretation itself. Machines no longer drive artists to obedient acceptance of their conditions; they are merely the tools of human creative power.

What is needed is a solution of the most difficult problem of all: how to record the power and volume of tone in a big orchestra, for instance, so that the

203

effect may not be entirely lost, even though reproduction takes place on inferior projector units.

The production of electrical resonance as such is
as little new as the device of the resonance chamber.
New effects are only achieved by the combination of
the three loudspeakers for the three sound-ranges.
This type of stereoscopic recording recalls the 'Wide
Range' reproduction technique of the Western Electric system in its division of the sound reproduced
into loudspeakers with higher, middle, and lower
pitches. But even these first-rate machines cannot
entirely make good the faults of an obsolete method
of recording.

To sum up, the possibilities of the new system of
electrical resonance with divided, adjustable sound-
range are as follows:

1. By setting the potentiometer accordingly, the
studio can for reverberation purposes be made as big
or as small as the number of performers or the character of the work demands.

2. The reverberation can be so controlled that
troublesome echoes are eliminated—for resonance
must not be confused with echo:

3. The sound recorded by the system in question does not fail of its effect even through primitive loudspeakers. Furthermore, the size and structure of the studio, in which reproduction takes place, is no longer a decisive factor.

4. From a purely musical point of view, (i) the sound of a full orchestra can be given as plastically as possible, and is not entirely lost even in faulty reproduction, since, by the regulation of the different pitches, a kind of gradated filtration of tone is achieved, and unnecessary and disturbing vibrations are excluded; (ii) soloists can, by the possible addition of further microphones, be made to stand out in plastic relief against their accompaniment, of whatever nature, whether music or incidental noises, and be safeguarded against blurred and 'booming' sounds.

Part Four: The Sound-film

B. The problem of acoustical control in the cinema

Once the whole process of sound-recording has been completed absolutely without fault, both artistically and technically, and granted that the reproduction units are likewise entirely beyond criticism, there finally remains the question of the acoustical state of the hall in which the performance takes place.

Complaints from all quarters, whether expert or lay, about faulty acoustics in cinemas are only too well grounded. Very many houses cannot do justice to the acoustical requirements of the sound-film. In most cases it is a question of uncorrected reverberation, which, it is imagined, could be regulated with a few curtains or similar primitive contrivances. But that is possible in only one or two instances. Almost every single sound-record differs from the rest in its acoustical effects. In their recording, sound-recordists have no standard for the sound-control in the cinema. So a standardisation of the reverberation period, and a constant control of the effects of echo, become equally necessary.

An additional consideration is that a number of halls are used not only for sound-film performances, but also for concerts and lectures, or even stage plays. And organs are built into almost all cinemas, involving recitals. In order to remedy the undesirable consequences which automatically attend non-observance of acoustical laws, C. W. Glover, an English sound-engineer, has suggested the installation of adjustable sound-absorbent panels. These can be noiselessly adjusted by the pressure of a switch, can be introduced in any room, and are calculated to regulate the reverberation time. In this way, the acoustical properties of an auditorium can be very simply altered. The economic value of halls is augmented, as no defective acoustics limit their uses.[1]

'No longer need the acoustics of a hall represent a compromise between optimum conditions for the respective uses to which the hall is liable,' says Glover very rightly. 'Every layman will recall halls where the reverberation was so strong that he could hardly understand what was said for so many echo effects. On the other hand, where reverberation is wholly absent, the sound is dry and brittle, without

[1]See article in 'Ideal Kinema and Studio', supplement to *Kinematograph Weekly*, May 1935.

life or colour. Defective acoustics are more noticeable with music than in the case of the spoken word.'

The fact that direct music even to-day still constitutes a considerable part of cinema programmes, gave Glover the idea of proposing the installation of variable absorbent panels, which are especially suitable for organ recitals, and can be regulated by the organist. Starting from the fact that the organist controls the sound of the instrument, there arises the possibility of inserting acoustical directions in the score, which would allow the player to command, not only the organ stops, but also the control of the auditorium acoustics, according to the composer's intentions. We can easily imagine what amazing effects could be obtained in this way.

One may say in general that for slow *tempi* reverberation time should be increased, and for quick *tempi* shortened. The reverberation periods can be calculated without difficulty, if we follow the metronome numbers given in many scores to convey accurately the pace of the music. It is especially advisable for true microphone recording that the interpretation of a passage of music should not be left too much scope for variation, and more attention be paid to the metronome directions. For the acoustical effects of sound-combinations alter immediately with every fluctuation of pace, and thus convey to the listener no exact idea of the composer's intentions.

Song of Ceylon by Basil Wright. Walter Leigh composed the music, which is illustrated opposite page 224

Alexander Korda's *Things to Come*. (The space gun.) Music by Arthur Bliss (see illustration facing page 218)

Recognising this, Glover sets out a classified time-table, in which, by tabulating side by side the *tempo*, the metronome number, the interval of a beat and of the ideal reverberation, he shows how easily a standardised reverberation time could be arrived at, applicable to all assembly halls:

Tempo	Maelzel Metronome beats per minute	Beat interval in secs.	Desirable Reverberation in secs.
Largo	40	1.50	3.00
	50	1.20	2.40
	60	1.00	2.00
	69		
Larghetto	70	0.86	1.72
	80	0.75	1.50
	90	0.67	1.34
	97		
Adagio	100	0.60	1.20
	110	0.55	1.10
	120	0.50	1.00
	126		
Andante	130	0.46	0.92
	140	0.43	0.86
	150 150	0.40	0.80
	160	0.38	0.76
Allegro			
	170	0.35	0.70
	180 180	0.33	0.66
Presto	190	0.32	0.64
	200	0.30	0.60
	208		

This table is equally important for the cinema architect and for the sound-recordist. If accurately applied, it guarantees the avoidance of overlapping of successive beats or words. As a general norm for the reverberation period Glover proposes that it should be approximately twice the duration of the beat. The ratio of loud and slow music to soft and quick music, expressed in numbers, should keep the same range in time, whatever factor be adopted: this ratio is 5-1, as the table shows.

Further directions by Glover: the rate of change of *tempo* is never so sudden that preparations cannot be made for it. 'Should the change be rapid and the time required to effect the change in reverberation considerable, a kind of acoustical overlap can be utilised. For adjusting the reverberation to suit a quickening of the *tempo*, the change should just precede the alteration in time, whereas if the change is in the other direction, the alteration in reverberation should just follow the change in *tempo*.'

Instruments like the piano with its pedals can obtain these effects by themselves. In electro-static musical instruments like the organ, the reverberation effects can be regulated by the player together with the stops. But most other instruments, and of course loudspeakers, cannot be adjusted and are therefore absolutely dependent on precise control of the auditorium acoustics. This should not be hard to carry out, if the above suggestions are put into effect.

4. Prominent European Film Composers and their artistic significance

It cannot come within the scope of this book to give complete biographical details about film composers of importance or an analysis of their works. The material is too varied and abundant, and completeness would be an almost unrealisable end. Nevertheless, this first attempt at a summary of all aspects of film music does call for an account of a number of typical figures, if it is to present a well-rounded impression of the whole subject. For this reason, there follow in the sections below a few brief notices, confined strictly to the main essentials, of those film composers who have, in the standard of their works, deserved well of the artistic film and its music.

But, even within this natural limitation, only a restricted selection could be made—one which has gone less by a man's name than by musical and general artistic criteria. The difficulties in obtaining the material, and lack of space, have had the inevitable result that many a fine musician has been left out of our list, whereby no judgment, adverse or otherwise, was at all intended.

The American film could not be considered at all within the framework of this book. Leaving men like Steiner, Newman, or Forbstein out of account, it is a fact that hitherto the artistic level of the American super-films (technically of such first-rate workmanship) has remained, apart from jazz, far more notable for its visual than for its musical achievements. The Americans are masters of compilation, even to-day. The originality that we find in their pictures, and occasionally also in their sound-construction, deserts them when it comes to music.

The other pole of world film production, Soviet Russia, can unfortunately only be touched on very briefly, because only a minimum selection of Russian films cross the Soviet frontiers, and further, because until recently there too, in that country possessed of the highest film culture, music lagged behind the level of the pictures. Only lately has a decided turn for the better become apparent, and this appears to be connected with the technical consolidation of Russian sound-recording equipment.

So we must confine ourselves in the main to the Central European and Western European countries, on the distinct understanding that this division into nations need not be identical with the passports of the composers concerned, but is only an indication of their artistic school and their chief field of activity till now.

Great Britain

In the period before the sound-film, no success attended the efforts made to create a British film industry which could work at a profit and produce good films. A great amount of capital was squandered in vain. The advent of the sound-film gave a new impetus to those unsuccessful attempts, but only in very recent years has what we may call the 'English film' come into being.

The activity of a man like Alexander Korda, who with his *Private Life of Henry VIII* gained a world-triumph for the first time for English films, coincides with the beginning of an era of successful work by the British film industry. Its first big achievements started about 1933. Further developments followed with astounding rapidity. The English did not fall into the error made by the French— they allowed prominent foreigners to take part in their films. In consequence, British films—at least, the super-films—shed their insular subjectivity, and became important, not only on the European, but also on the North American Continent.

This fact was decisive: a British film production with a North American outlet for its pictures was bound to outstrip all its competitors in Europe. It involves a close co-operation between London and Hollywood, the centre of American film production. Provided that British films succeed in developing further in point of art and technique on the lines which have been followed hitherto, they will, together with America, gain supremacy, not only in Europe, but in the whole world. The film is indeed, in the nature of its whole economic structure, an organism whose best and most expensive products only begin to pay their way in the *international* market.

If therefore the British authorities remain as hitherto tolerant of a certain percentage of foreign labour among the home personnel, and thus maintain the *international* value of British films (films for home consumption are in any case produced in ample abundance), then we may safely assume that the London studios will continue in the future to play a decisive part in the artistic development of the film.

After this digression, which was inevitable in this section on British film music, let us return to music itself. It appears to be developing with all the greater rapidity, as London musical life, even outside the films, has become one of the most intensely active in the world. London, as a world music-centre, naturally

Facsimile of a score page of Arthur Benjamin's
music for the film *Wharves and Strays*.

exerts an influence on those kinds of music which lie outside its concert-halls and opera-houses. What is in many cases lacking is not so much technical experience as the recognition of the significance of film music for the form, content, and effect of a film.

One of the first original scores for British sound-films was composed in 1933 by Clarence Raybould, then a Professor at the Guildhall School of Music in London, for Paul Rotha's documentary film *Rising Tide*. Although at that time British film music had as yet had no experience to guide it, this score nevertheless does, even in retrospect, possess certain value. The more important works by British film composers only begin shortly after that date.

Prominent among them as an expert we may place Arthur Benjamin. He was born in 1893 in Sydney. At 17 years of age, he came to London, won a scholarship at the Royal College of Music, and there studied composition and pianoforte. After the interruption caused by the War, in which he was an airman, and was shot down and made prisoner, he taught piano for another three years at the State Conservatory in Sydney, returned to England once more, and won the Carnegie Prize for a string quartet—the first work he published.

Since then, his reputation has steadily grown. He composed two successful one-act operas, several orchestral works, chamber. music, and songs. He teaches piano at the Royal College of Music, and he has composed the music for a number of prominent films, in which he has proved his sense of film-musical forms, his artistic taste in composition, and his understanding of the needs of the microphone to an ever-increasing degree. Judging by the music for films like *The Man who Knew Too Much*, *The Clairvoyant*, *The Guv'nor*, *The Scarlet Pimpernel*, *Wharves and Strays*, *The Turn of the Tide*, he ranks to-day among the most experienced and skilful composers in the youthful British film industry.

An excellent orchestrator, he very soon realised that microphonic scores must differ from traditional symphonic tone-combinations. He had the courage to give effect to his conclusions in action: he dared to depose the strings from their supremacy, reducing them to the level of mere filling-in parts, and no longer, or only very seldom, allowing them the melody (see musical facsimile). He uses saxophones for the *ripieno* of the horns, avoids the use of the kettle-drum wherever possible, and renders the *pizzicato* of the double-basses on the piano or on the tuba. He regards the flute as a real solo instrument for the microphone. He considers it unnecessary to use an orchestra of more than about twenty players, and he is right: well-orchestrated music needs no mammoth body of players.

Benjamin's musical style is clear and simple. He

writes no really modern music, but by no means leaves the experience of modern music out of consideration. He knows very well how to blend into one uniform texture the style of a film, the public's perceptive faculty, and his own knowledge of artistic effects, whether in harmony, counterpoint, or instrumentation.

He, like all other film musicians who are accustomed to write music outside their film connection, suffers as a result of the deficient time-arrangements organised by the producing staff: these people have not even now been able to bring themselves to rate the importance of music high enough, and therefore to give the composer time enough for a more careful study of the score.

Besides him, there are in the field to-day two other serious composers, though it is true that until recently neither of them had the actual experience needed for the film and the microphone: Arthur Bliss and William Walton.

Bliss belongs to the generation of modern British symphonic composers after Elgar, who, like Vaughan Williams and Arnold Bax, have remained amazingly young and up to date. His first film, *Things to Come*, written by H. G. Wells, shows an undoubted sense for film effects and the emphasis of pictorial ideas. His orchestra, a big symphony orchestra, has not yet managed to free itself from the symphonic tradition (see musical facsimile). But the microphone is indeed a problem which even the most prominent musicians have to solve for themselves in practice. In future scores Bliss too will no doubt revise his style. Almost all composers who derive from the symphony or the opera only learn with reluctance, and at the cost of many difficulties, what limitations they must set themselves—on their music paper—for the sake of the microphone. Perhaps this book can do something to save future film composers these first hurdles in their experience.

Bliss has also arranged the music for this film as a concert-suite, which was performed with success at the Queen's Hall and undoubtedly won many new friends for film music. The idea of performing good film scores, as formally complete and not merely descriptive pieces of music pure and simple, should indeed be recognised far more than has hitherto been the case.

Like Bliss, William Walton, who may be described as England's Hindemith, is a beginner at film music. Yet he showed by his music for the Bergner film *Escape Me Never* how much feeling he has for atmosphere (see musical quotation). The haste in which he was forced to compose this music, and the good result which in spite of everything attended its performance, indicate clearly how great an improvement he will achieve in future works (in *As you like*

Score page of Arthur Bliss's music for the film
Things to Come. (Facsimile.)

it, for example), if he is allowed more time and leisure to do justice to a field of activity to which he is still a stranger. After the completion of his big symphony, the enthusiastic reception of which set him overnight in the front rank of representative modern British composers, he began to study the sound-film on the spot, in the studio; and it is to be hoped that he will be among its future artistic promoters.

He too has been converted to the principle of a small orchestra, although he has not given up the strings as basis of his instrumentation. As a conscientious artist, who does not like working for the moment alone, but wants his creations to have a lasting value, Walton is, like so many of his colleagues, troubled by the fact that films disappear so quickly, and with them all their value. But we should not believe that things of real worth in a film disappear, if they *are* actually there. They make first of all an impression on the public, and then have a beneficial effect on future productions. Moreover, we must not forget that a successful film is seen and heard in a relatively short period by many more people than, for instance, a symphonic work in decades. And after all we must face facts: the film is unchangeably rooted in the present. It is a kind of performance which is always extremely limited by the time factor. Only in most exceptional cases is a film that has once finished its round of the markets revived again and again, like *Dr. Caligari*. But even in the files it is not forgotten.

Eugene Goossens, another leading English musician, has so far only in one film, *The Constant Nymph*, shown that his style can adapt itself to film purposes. He now lives in the United States, and is probably lost to British film production for the present. Beckett Williams, who is at one and the same time politician, writer, and musician, has evolved some interesting views on film music in a few short films, such as *Kamet Conquered*, and in a series of articles on theory.

It is not to be wondered at that some of the most talented musicians of the younger generation in Great Britain turned their attention to that sphere of film production which, of all the work of the London studios, was far the most interesting—the documentary film as a work of art. When Basil Wright's *Song of Ceylon* won the first prize for documentary films at the Brussels International Film Competition in 1935, it began to dawn upon the world across the Channel that here some exemplary work on behalf of this very important branch of film production was being done by independently-minded young artists and engineers in London.

Under the leadership of John Grierson, British documentary films have in a few years attained a level to which neither American productions nor

Page from the music by William Walton for the
film *Escape Me Never*.

those of the rest of Europe—with the exception perhaps of Russia—can aspire. As film officer to the
G.P.O. film unit, Grierson has Government support,
and so is no longer dependent on the varying moods
and fancies of commercially-minded film magnates.
This G.P.O. unit and the group gathered round Paul
Rotha are to-day first-class craftsmen in their mental
grasp of their material and in their understanding of
the needs of sound and picture and of sound-film construction. Men like Wright, Cavalcanti, and Rotha
(whose careful textbook *Documentary Film* should be
read by everyone who wishes to know anything about
the purpose, form, technique, and social implications
of the documentary film), have founded a school
which is years in advance of normal film production.

No wonder, therefore, that young composers who
refuse to tread well-worn paths and, at the beginning of their artistic development, seek to overcome
the dead weight of tradition, welcome with enthusiasm the chance to work under such ideal conditions,
even though their fees may not run into many figures. Two of them, for example, Benjamin Britten
and Walter Leigh, have proved themselves real experts in forming the musical elements of a film into
universal representations of sound. Their film music
transcends the score of musical notes and absorbs
within itself the sound of real life (in a stylised
form), whether it be of single voices, of choruses, or

of natural noises, by turning it to music and giving it rhythm.

Let us consider Britten. He is one of the youngest of the modern generation of British musicians, a composer of serious chamber music no less than of film sound-strips. In the G.P.O. film *Coal Face*, an exceedingly searching pictorial survey of Great Britain's most important industry, he formed such a unity of music, words spoken in chorus, and stylised noises. It is astonishing to observe how, with the most scanty material, using only a piano and a speaking chorus, he can make us dispense gladly with realistic sounds. This stylisation makes a much stronger impression than a normal musical accompaniment. The commentator's explanations are cut to extreme brevity and are limited to such information as by its content may knit the connection between the sound-groups still more closely together. The atmosphere of the dark world of the work in the mines, the grim monotony of the miners' hard life, but, notwithstanding, the vital importance of that work, exclude any lyric feeling. The rhythms of this life are hard; hard likewise is the music and its interweaving with the speaking choruses. The general atmosphere of the film is dark, and its music neither makes it brighter nor does it underline the shadows superfluously. In a word, the power-ratio between picture and music is always most ideally balanced.

Leigh's accompaniment to the *Song of Ceylon* was composed in quite a different way, but no less perfectly. Here the film was cut after the music, and so it is that the single sections of pure music show a clear and rounded form. Leigh—like Britten, a young composer of the modern school—has also realised that the sound-film, a new art, requires a new musical technique. His music departs from tradition, not only in its form, in connection with the tonality of the whole film; his instrumentation also displays in its transparent economy a striking understanding of the special requirements of the microphone. Wind, above all wood-wind, dominate in delicate contrapuntal sound-texture, even in combination with strings, used solo. The score of the *Song of Ceylon* are a practical illustration of the theses put forward in this book: they point the path which real film music has to follow (see musical facsimile). Rotha, in *Documentary Film*, also very rightly laid emphasis on this very same work by Leigh.

It is indeed greatly to be desired that the influence of these young pioneers of British documentary films should spread farther. That would assure us of at least one reservoir of film art in Europe, besides the springs of Russian cinematographic art, which might continue and replace in a more sensible and more logical way the pioneer experiments of the former Parisian group, and generally become a source of inspiration for the industry as a whole.

The short time during which British film studios have played a more important rôle in world production has seen a number of British musicians won over to the cause of the film. They are furthering the development of their art beyond the frontiers of their country, and they compare very favourably with their Continental contemporaries, who are the subjects of the following sections.

Germany

Germany, once the country of musicians *par excellence*, has produced a host of film musicians, or at least till 1933 afforded them such creative possibilities as enabled them to make a significant contribution to the solution of the problems connected with the film and its music.

One of the most outstanding among them is Dr. Karol Rathaus, an Austrian by birth, but a former pupil of Schreker, who received his artistic training in the musical circles of Berlin, which once exercised such an influence on the whole trend of modern music. Thus his works can very well be classed with those of the German school.

Rathaus published a great number of works for the stage, symphonic scores, and chamber music. He

Facsimile of a page from Walter Leigh's music for
Song of Ceylon. This is a very good example of effective microphone orchestration.

is a master of the art of phrasing and instrumentation. He belongs to the type of intellectual musician,
and that is probably why his keen artistic perception
enabled him to grasp the essentials of film music in
his very first score for the films, the first-rate music
which accompanied Ozep's film *Karamazov*. This
score can be regarded as a model of film-symphonic
art, and even to-day is still actually exemplary in its
form, its rhythm which follows the course of the
picture, and its success in seizing the atmosphere of
Dostoievsky's masterpiece.

Rathaus' film compositions are not equal in musical value, but they are all designed with great intellectual assurance: *Hallo! Paris, Die 13 Koffer des
Herrn O. F.*[1], *City Nights* (a film which was pictorially
on a much lower level than the music), and *Amok*,
in the last of which the line of the *Karamazov* style
was carried further and consolidated. In London he
composed *The Dictator*.

It is interesting to see how an artist like Rathaus
solves the problem of the song hit in sound-films. In
his work it becomes the symphonic pivot, and as
such it hardly attracts attention at all. He fuses it
organically within the line of the whole work, so that
it does not stand out in undeserved prominence, as is
generally the case. This style very happily combines
a modern diction with transparency of writing,

[1]= 'The 13 Trunks of Mr. O. F.'

absolutely intelligible melody, and at the same time an intense mental penetration into the meaning of the plot. There is no bar that has not its justification, no phrase that is merely superficial.

But probably the most characteristic factor in Rathaus' film works, apart from their compactness of form, is the coincidence in rhythm between picture and music. It is true that in his most important creations he had the luck to enjoy the co-operation of a director like Fedor Ozep, who concedes to music a position in accord with its significance and is prepared to cut big scenes to conform with the already completed and recorded music. Thus the composer could create a form complete in itself on the basis of the pictures already taken, and this form was regarded as the foundation of the final structure to be attained after cutting. This is, especially in musical films, for which the pictures and the music are not recorded in parallel, certainly one of the best, most vivid, and artistically most acceptable solutions for musical scenes.

Paul Dessau has not been so fortunate in his directors. At least, not in the case of the man for whom he managed to write his most considerable scores—Arnold Fanck, who is not musical and has no developed sense of rhythm. Fanck, to whom the film owes a number of excellent Alpine and snow pictures, is so exclusively a man of eye that, when all is said, he works in the technique of silent films. So it inevitably happened that the compactness of Dessau's scores was very often impaired by Fanck's unsympathetic and callous cutting. It is all the more to the composer's credit that his works still retained their intrinsic value.

Dessau, a composer of symphonic and chamber music, conductor at the Cologne and Berlin Operas, went over to the films a short time before the advent of sound-films. As permanent conductor in a large Berlin cinema palace, he already attracted attention in those early days by his audacity in illustration, and also by some admirable original compositions to accompany silent films (such as a Suite for Starewitch's doll film, *The Magic Clock*). When the sound-films came, he directed the musical treatment of several films starring the tenor Richard Tauber, wrote the music for E. A. Dupont's *Salto Mortale*, and then composed for the best known of the Fanck films, *Storm over Mont Blanc, Der Weisse Rausch, Engadine Adventure, S.O.S. Iceberg*. These were his masterpieces, and they all evidence a very expert hand, and a strong understanding for atmosphere, though they are not always free from a coolness which is sometimes too objective. A theme like that of the Iceberg film (see musical quotation) gives some idea of the standard of his musical composition.

In contrast with Rathaus' intellectuality, Dessau

is the less prejudiced musician, and this occasionally tempted him to miss his musical cue in some passages for sheer joy in carrying the musical line to its logical conclusion.

Like Rathaus, Dessau uses the traditional symphony orchestra. He belongs to those composers who, in defiance of the requirements of the microphone, worked with a strong body of string-players. However great the transparency with which his music is orchestrated, owing to its string parts it does not fall within the category of microphonic music proper.

If Rathaus and Dessau, at least as regards orchestration, represent the symphonic tradition, Hanns Eisler was probably the first man to make a radical departure from it. A composer of oratorios, orchestral works, and songs of militant socialistic content, he wrote a piece of music, as early as 1927, when the sound-film did not yet officially exist in Europe at all, for an experimental film, *Opus 3*, by W. Ruttmann, which received its first performance at the Baden-Baden Music Festival in that year. Eisler, by the way, was one of the earliest composers to try and create music intrinsically suited to wireless transmission.

With his accompaniment to Victor Trivas' *War is Hell*, a splendid film, which unfortunately long failed to receive the appreciation due to it in Central Europe,

Musical quotation from *S O S Iceberg*. Theme sketch by
Paul Dessau. Facsimile.

he established himself in the foremost rank of modern creative film composers.

This score was new from more than one point of view: in its rhythm, its form, and its orchestration. All those who saw, heard, and understood this film, will never forget how the movement and dynamics of the scenes in *War is Hell* were musically interpreted, and how extraordinary the effect of such harmony between music and picture proved to be. The musical expert was struck, not only by the compact form, but also by the remarkable success in the technical construction of every single passage. Great instrumental artistry was here subordinated to film needs. (The most prominent items of this score were often performed in the form of a concert suite.)

Similar, if not quite such striking effects were achieved by Eisler in Dudow's *Kuhle Wampe*, and the falling off in the musical impression is more the fault of the producer than of the director. A scherzo in beautifully constructed counterpoint—the scene of the cyclists running a race to win employment (already described on p. 156) is in its forceful line worthy of comparison with any symphonic concert item.

A work in Russia, *Konsomol*, and the film *New Earth*, both produced by the Dutchman Ivens, are little known outside the Soviet Union; two French films, turned in Paris, *Dans les rues* (Victor Trivas) and *Le grand jeu* (Jean Feyder), successfully

229

carry on the individual tendency of his work. Admittedly they soften the composer's style, conditioned as they are by the attitude of Western European production, but they in no way impair his originality. Eisler also worked for the Elstree studios: he wrote the music for *Abdul the Damned*.

The characteristic quality of Eisler's film music is, for the most part, due to the orchestra which he created for the microphone. Even before the advent of the sound-film, Eisler was a musician for social reform, openly despising art for art's sake, a fervent adherent of modern music on a collective basis, that is, folk-music, popular and school music. Perhaps we may thus explain (psychologically as well) his *aversion to the employment of strings*, which mute rather than soften any hardness. Eisler's most original line later on, strangely enough, conformed exactly with the needs of the microphone; and so he could retain it with trifling modifications. His intellectual consistency and artistic austerity are in accord with the fact that everything purely illustrative, giving colour and iridescence, in short, impressionistic, cannot last. The film composer must, according to him, develop a highly individualistic style for the sake of the films' reality, without any consequential sacrifice of the originality of the writing.

We may maintain that Eisler fulfils these requirements of his in his own writings. His scores are not-

230

Typical example of a film score by Hanns Eisler (without stringed instruments). Facsimile of the original MS. from the music for the film *La nouvelle terre*.

able for their unequivocal character, which is an example to others. It may be regarded as symbolical of the correctness of his judgment of the development of sound-film and film music, that his realistic instrumentation harmonised with technical requirements in orchestration due to the microphone.

It is very regrettable that Paul Hindemith, after an experimental film *Vormittagsspuk*, which was first performed in Baden-Baden in the year 1929, never again had occasion to work for the films; yet this musician, readily receptive to everything new, the most prominent of the young generation of German composers, occupied himself with the problems of film music (admittedly in a fairly unmethodical and not always technically correct form) in a course of lectures organised by himself at the Berlin Academy of Music.

Kurt Weill, also, after his initial experiences with the *Dreigroschenoper* score, kept away from the films. The dictatorial force of the chiefs of film companies did not suit his uncompromising nature; their views on film music did not coincide with his, and so he brought an indictment on the issue, which resulted in a trial conducted with considerable violence. Ernst Toch, also one of the most interesting figures in modern music in pre-Hitlerite Germany, only began in 1933-34, in London, to busy himself with the problems of film music. He and Weill now appear to have chosen the U.S.A. as the prospective scene of their activities.

As a type of the conciliatory popular musician we may mention Wolfgang Zeller, who is approximately the German counterpart of the Italian Giuseppe Becce. Zeller composed two of the first German super sound-films, Ruttmann's *Melodie der Welt* and *Das Land ohne Frauen*. Zeller's music is naturally conceived, intellectually simple, always adapted to the needs of the moment, illustrative in the romantic sense, and extremely easily understood by the broad masses. It adds nothing new, and never—apart from a some-times rather lachrymose tone—makes a disturbing impression.

Zeller, besides his bigger film dramas, composed a whole series of cultural pictures and expedition films, and in this connection we may emphasise the fact that there is in his scores no false drawing-room exoticism, such as one was frequently forced to hear, in the period before the sound-film, performed by cinema orchestras.

Among composers of the comic Muse, who need not always be the reverse of serious, Mischa Spoli-ansky and Friedrich Holländer are especially worthy of note. Spoliansky, who is now working in London and has written two such excellent scores as those for Zoltan Korda's *Sanders of the River* and René Clair's *The Ghost goes West*, is one of the few jazz

composers who know how to intellectualise jazz. He
can write in popular style, without becoming vulgar.
His musical comedies always had distinction, and in
many cases the music was superior to the film for
which he composed. Now he has been given the
chance in London of working with an artist like Clair.
In this score some lengthy passages which are purely
symphonic prove that the song-hit composer Spoliansky has to be taken seriously in the rôle of serious
composer as well.

Friedrich Holländer, who is now working in
Hollywood, likewise helped to revive the form of
sound-film operetta, and more especially contrived
the growth of the theme-song out of the rhythm of
the picture and the scenario in a manner which is
altogether worthy of imitation. At a very considerable distance behind these two musicians, there are
composers like Paul Abraham, Werner R. Heymann,
Franz Léhar, Robert Stolz, and others who cannot
really be described as film composers, even though
they are, like Heymann, clever musicians and have
composed a great number of successful films. Their
style is and will remain operetta style, which is, as we
have seen, impossible to transfer directly to the sound-
film.

France

The situation of film music in France is not the same as it was (formerly) in Germany. The prominent French composers are as a rule much more conservative, and in their typically French individualism disinclined on principle to practise the mechanical arts. There are only a few really great musicians in France who have grasped and appropriated to themselves the meaning of the new art-form which has arisen in the sound-film, or even the idea of the microphone. And one of the most eminent among them, Arthur Honegger, is Swiss by birth.

He may to-day be regarded as the true leader of modern film music in France. This man, whose great work as a composer of 'absolute' music has won him a world-wide reputation, by the artistic influence centred in his person, became one of the most valuable supporters of the movement to gain recognition for film music in France and the rest of the world.

His activities in connection with the film have so far not been very extensive in quantity, but they are none the less important for that. The mighty trilogy of *Les Misérables* by Raymond Bernard is outstanding because of its effectiveness with audiences. After

it comes *Rapt* by Kirzanov, a score which derived
especial musical significance from the director's
sympathetic attitude. In a special number of the
Revue Musicale, of Paris, which is devoted to sound-
films and film music, Honegger himself published a
few comments on his compositions, explaining in a
highly interesting manner his method of going to
work and his attitude to special problems. (*Revue
Musicale*, Paris, December 1934.)

In *Cessez le feu* the master reveals himself as a
song composer, and thus admits the validity of
Eisler's theory that the film composer must command every style. Especially valuable for the films is
the musical version of the remarkable Bartosch-
Maserel film *L'idée*, which is probably one of the
best film scores Honegger has written. One of his
latest works is the music for Dostoievsky's *Crime et
Châtiment*.

This artist's musical diction does not fail of its
usual energy and clarity when he sets to work on a
film score. Nevertheless, he subordinates himself to
his material with a degree of insight that is altogether amazing. What is perhaps most admirable of
all, he always strikes an idiom which even that section of his public which is not so well educated musically (in films this class has always to be reckoned
with) can still understand, without abandoning his
own specific and very characteristic style in the pro-

cess. He works, like Rathaus and Eisler, in forms complete in themselves and uniform in rhythm. His orchestra, always a chamber orchestra, is treated as a combination of soloists; the strings are not omitted, but are very weakly represented.

Honegger's music always sounds clear and un-equivocal in films and elsewhere. The melodic lines are set against one another with great contrapuntal artistry, their periods so chosen that they can be re-produced in a plastic form.

France's other prominent musician, Darius Mil-haud, in spite of all his sympathy for the film, has a far stronger inner shyness of it than Honegger: the latter after all worked even for the silent film (the Abel Gance films) at a time when it did not in the least pay the 'serious' musician to busy himself with the art of film.

In Milhaud's first sound-film score for Caval-canti's *Petite Lili*, one of the experimental films performed in Baden-Baden in 1929, he succeeded in making a song the illustrative focus of the music. Af-ter the success of this first effort, four years passed before the composition of Richter's *Hallo, Every-body!* and Renoir's *Madame Bovary*, the latter a film in which the music was concentrated entirely on portraying the atmosphere. In point of rhythm, this abortive film version of Flaubert's masterpiece had little to say for itself. A series of pieces from this version appeared in an arrangement for piano in the *Edition du Cinéma,* Paris. They reveal the sensitive feeling of the subject, which in the film strayed from the psychological to the sentimental, interpreted by a musician speaking in terms of modern music, the composer of *Christopher Columbus.*

In Bernard's *Tartarin de Tarascon* this line of development is continued. Milhaud, too, still employs strings, in a very transparent orchestra. His music sounds plastically in reproduction, yet it achieves all the more powerful effect, the more independence it displays, and the less it is subordinated to the film in its construction. To this extent Milhaud does not yet belong to those composers who are able to give a new impetus to film music. His scores as such are first-rate, but they always either remain somewhat alien to the film they accompany, or, if they attempt to defer entirely to it, possess a paler quality than is usually found in Milhaud's compositions. On the other hand, the music with the scenes in his opera-oratorio *Christopher Columbus* which are resolved in the medium of the film, is superlative.

What has been said of Milhaud, can equally well be said of another serious composer: Jacques Ibert's work is musically on a very high plane, but he has hitherto rather held aloof from the films, and so cannot be described as a vital film composer. Maurice Jaubert, on the other hand, who composed the music

for René Clair's *Quatorze juillet*, is well on the way
to the front rank among French film composers. His
musical accompaniments to the documentary films,
La vie d'un fleuve by Lods, and Storck's *Easter Is-
land*, may be described as the most interesting modern French film scores after Honegger. Jaubert's
music is at times not devoid of a certain banality,
but almost always shows a strong insight into the
rhythm and atmosphere of the pictures.

Henri Sauguet and, above all, Georges Auric are
also important. Like Milhaud, the latter was at one
time a member of the famous 'Six', to whom credit
is due for any reforms that have taken place in
French music.

Auric has made himself known by his music for
René Clair's film *A nous la liberté*. In collaboration
with the gifted director, he suceeded not only in
capturing the desired musical atmosphere, but, what
is a still greater achievement, in giving a fitting musical finish to the type of musical film developed by
Clair—following the selfsame principles which we
laid down in the section on the various forms of
musical sound-film. Here it is less a question of
purely musical values than of the tonal finish of the
dramatic entity. Auric is the converse of Milhaud:
one of those composers whose adaptability to the film
is greater than the value of their music.

Of Sauguet we so far only know the music for

l'Herbier's *L'Epervier*. We can see that here are great possibilities for the future; and it is one of the many mysteries surrounding the French film industry that this talented composer has been given so few chances to show his worth.

The comic Muse is represented in France by composers like Georges van Parys (the composer of Clair's *Le Million* and several Parisian films of lesser significance), Raoul Moretti (the composer of *Sous les toits de Paris*), the gifted Michel Levine, Jean Wiener, and finally Reynaldo Hahn, an especially versatile and clever musician. They all command a simple and graceful mode of writing, without however covering any new ground. None of them has managed to excel Holländer's or Spoliansky's ventures. But, on the other hand, it must be admitted that they reach a far higher standard of taste than the German composers in all problems connected with the theme-song.

Italy

Film music was first raised to the status of a definite concept by an Italian, Giuseppe Becce. He was born in Padua as the son of a family steeped in music, and first studied philosophy and music in his native city, then took his degree there, and actually took up his residence as professor.

239

But in those days he saw no prospects of rising higher in his native land. The outside world beckoned, and the reputation of pre-War Berlin as an aspiring city of art attracted him enormously. He intended to continue his studies at Berlin University, but his passion for music thwarted these plans. In any case, he went to Berlin and fell on evil days. He waited for the performance of an opera and a symphony. (The opera, *The Couch of Madame Dubarry*, was later performed in Bremen.) And then, by an odd coincidence, he happened on the films.

The librettist of his opera was assistant director to Oscar Messter, who at this time was about to make a big film about Wagner, and was searching desperately for a musically-minded man to take the part of the genius of Bayreuth. When the librettist drew his attention to Becce, they looked for him and found him in a café, paid his bill, and dragged him straightway to the studio. Becce at first refused to accompany them, because he thought that they were creditors who had lost all patience. . . .

In the studio, after a short audition, he was not only taken on for the chief part, but also engaged to compose the music for the film. Wagner's works were at that time still protected by copyright, and so his own music could not be used. This became the first original composition written for a film. Fate ordained that the work, which to him was a pointer to his new career, made film history. His first-rate theoretical knowledge and his talent in conducting (he was a pupil of Nikisch) furnished a solid foundation for his new occupation as film musician.

Becce has composed such a huge number of silent and sound films that we can only quote just a few of the most important here. His sound-films include: *The Favourite of Schönbrunn*; the Trenker films *Son of the White Mountains, Mountains in Flames, The Rebel, The Lost Son*; the Riefenstahl film, *The Blue Light*; the Fanck film, *The King of Mont Blanc*; and the Machaty film, *Ecstasy*. In addition, there are countless works composed for cartoon and documentary films.

Of all composers, Becce has undoubtedly written the most for films. The number of his compositions for silent films, the *Kinotheks*, is astonishingly big. His music ever retains its attractive and popular quality, and can be understood by even the most primitive of listeners. Songs and serenades of his have run into edition after edition.

There are many musicians and musical experts who find Becce's music too naïve, and regard it as insipid and insignificant. Now Becce was never a composer of such profundity as, for instance, a Rathaus or a Honegger, and probably never seriously claimed to be so. His talent for film music is founded, not so much on the special evolution of an idea, as on the structure of his music, contained in a slight framework, adaptable and yet always dramatically effective. He was the first man to give the film a practical style in music. He actually was able, during the transitional period between silent and sound films, to eke some possibilities out of illustration by gramophone records. And he was among the first, long before Disney, to show how cartoon films should be composed. It is very probable that the Americans were inspired by his music for cartoons (for *Felix the Cat* and *Oswald*) to the musical development of such films as the Mickey Mouse series, which to-day are the delight of the whole world.

Becce's sound-film compositions set no problems, plumb no great depths, are in style related perhaps to Italian opera—but they almost always take in the pith and core of their subject. They are in this respect at least to be preferred to works by more pretentious composers, who despise the film in their hearts, but for the sake of the fee condescend to work for it, and then compose without reference to the pictures or even kill them with their score, instead of co-ordinating the two factors or adapting their creations to the purpose in hand.

A study of Becce's works for films, beginning with his first *Kinotheks*, would be something worth recommending to every aspiring film musician, even though he may already have a dozen concert pieces to his name. That is why Becce's name will for ever be bound up with the history of the film.

Becce has remained Italian, although he has lived in Berlin for a generation. He did not even fall a prey to the artistic influences of his adopted land. Perhaps that is the deepest psychological reason why of all men a musician of his kind had to become the pioneer of film music, and not one of those *Weltanschauung* composers, who would certainly not have worked intuitively enough to evolve the facility necessary to the film-musical form.

Italy has also produced more modern composers, though unfortunately they have had all too few opportunities, owing to limited Italian film production, to venture into the sphere of the film; yet, where they have done work, they have trodden new paths. Vittorio Rieti, for instance, famous and respected in the province of serious music, in 1932 composed a film *O la borsa, o la vita* and attempted in this score, like Eisler, to attack the problem of the microphone by a new kind of orchestral combination. As the example of a page of his score shows, it involves the complete wind parts of a symphony orchestra, supplemented by saxophones and piano, but without violins and violas: only 2 violoncellos and 2 double-basses are included. Rieti's first work for the film is gifted and interesting; let us hope that it will not be the last.

Extremely interesting is Francesco Malipiero's

score for Ruttmann's film *Accaio*, which was made in Italy. The distinguished composer has here displayed his artistic instinct in his first important work for the film.

Soviet Russia

The Russian film has for years been among the most intriguing phenomena of the world's film output. The advent of the sound-film only managed for a short period to arrest this state of affairs. The Russian sound-film came into being, and the few proofs of its existence, which the rest of Europe has been allowed to see, go to show that the great traditions of Russian silent-film production are being worthily upheld.

Strangely enough, music at the outset could not keep pace with these unique achievements in the technique of the *mise-en-scène* and photo-construction. For years, Tschaikovsky's style determined the *genre* of Russian film music, and it was not until quite recently that a few young composers, among them especially D. Shostakovitch, tried to give things a new turn. His achievements are not the only factor which justify the assumption that this country is also about to solve the problem of film music, both serious and light, in a form which will correspond in quality to its pictures.

Example of the music for the Italian film *O la borsa, o la vita,* composed by Vittorio Rieti (no violins or violas!).

Shostakovitch has for example written a notable score for the film *Shame* (*Counterplan*), which gives hearers not a few novelties in rhythm and in tonality. The use of electrical instruments and special sound-effects interwoven with the music presents quite new sensations to the ear.

In the less serious style, Alexandrov has shown conclusively, in the first Russian *Jazz Comedy*, that even jazz is not beyond the capacity of Moscow's artists.

There can be no doubt, after these first successful attempts, that the musical vacuum which has often provoked the experts to helpless amazement will now very soon be destroyed once for all.

Part Five: Training the Rising Generation

.

On the establishment of a
Microphone Academy

The new evolution of the 'mechanical' arts can no longer tolerate the gigantic dilettantism from which they have suffered, especially in the case of the film. On the contrary, it calls for a more highly systematic and painstaking exploration of their individual departments by research workers, teachers, and students than has been known before.

Added to this, there is the necessity for a methodical training of the rising generation. It will no longer do that young people who wish to work as musicians for the film should begin their job without the requisite specialised knowledge, so that, if they are lucky, after some years they may say that they have learnt *by experience* (that is, their own mistakes). If this procedure is followed, no good will come of it, either for young artists or for the industry. And as for gradual progress or building on the shoulders of those who have gone before, that will be altogether out of the question.

249

The urgency of a well-planned and systematic education is becoming all the greater as the microphonic arts extend their influence. The microphone to-day has three functions—sound-film, radio, and gramophone recording—and the separation of these three provinces of art could only be fraught with harmful consequences, because a very close connection exists between them. It therefore becomes the duty of research and of pedagogy to treat these three categories conjointly.

The experimental venture of a comprehensive academy dealing with the microphone, planned in Berlin in the year 1932 on the basis of my ideas, but later, for various reasons, not realised in practice, was already very near a solution of the problem. But, before we treat the establishment of this Microphone Academy in greater detail, it may be appropriate to recall the experiments made by the earliest schools of film music, as they already existed, in Berlin alone, in the days of the silent film. Here again a knowledge of this historical evolution will bring us nearer to recognition of the cogency of the question.

The two big conservatories which were of importance besides the State Academy of Music, namely, the Stern Conservatory and the Klindworth-Scharwenka Conservatory, started classes in film music in the year 1929. In the Klindworth-Scharwenka, practical experiments were made in a projection-room specially built for the purpose. In the Stern, the first course of systematic lectures on film music was given in the winter of 1929-30. In its second part, this course took note, even at that early date, of the newly discovered sound-film. The syllabus of that first term in film music, the lectures for which I had the honour to deliver, is even to-day not without interest when we look back on it:

FIRST PART
Introduction to film music
  The history of its evolution;
  Nature and definition of the expression 'film music'.
  The complete sphere of film music, as it is today:
    With silent films, played by a living orchestra;
    Illustration (compilation); use of music from existing literature and the *Kinothek*;
    Original composition.
    With silent films, in the form of mechanical reproduction (gramophone records):
    Compilation;
    Composition.
  General remarks on the aesthetics of film music:
    From the point of view of art;
    As regards culture (the public and film music).

SECOND PART
Practical use of music with the silent film
  The cinema orchestra and its material:
    Instruments employed, problems of the parts to be included, arrangements.
    Illustration, and the causes of its predominance:
    Its technique in relation to the dramaturgy of the film; line and cutting; general questions of dramatic construction.

The musical technique of illustration:

Utilisation of existing music, *Kinotheks*; the technique of transitions; the scope of musical dramaturgy in the film.

Joint visit to a film, after prior discussion of the musical structure of the illustration concerned.

Original composition for the silent film:

Technique of its composition, and creation out of the spirit and the dramatic texture of the pictures; its musical resources; the co-operation between composer, author, and producer.

Mechanical music with the silent film:

Its development, and the various systems;

Technical and artistic possibilities for compilation and composition;

Joint visit to a gramophone-recording studio for a performance and explanation of a film illustrated by record reproduction.

The problem of synchronisation in the silent film:

Former and present-day inventions.

THIRD PART

Practical use of music with the sound-film

Nature of the sound-film, its possibilities, and its two systems (sound-on-disc and sound-on-film).

Recording and synchronising technique:

Theoretical; and practical (a visit to a synchronising studio).

Musical illustration with the sound-film.

Original composition for the sound-film:

Technique of its composition, and its instrumentation.

Problem of instruments for microphone reproduction:

Microphone instruments; microphone scores.

FOURTH PART

Prospects

Joint visit to a sound-film, after a preliminary discussion of its music. Subsequent critical debate.

Establishment of a microphone academy

Practical seminary
 Studies in illustration, with a small film as the patient;
 Attempts at composition;
 Exercises in instrumentation and arrangements;
 Performance of the best compositions by an orchestra
  composed of students, with a film projected at the same
  time.

The rapid ascent of the sound-film, however, necessitated a change in the method of teaching, and demanded the comprehensive study of all the microphonic arts. In this respect, too, events in Berlin furnish interesting examples.

There were never studios for gramophone-recording. The firms interested were content to collect experience in their own laboratories. Any progress which was made was due less to artistic activity than to the results of electro-acoustical science. Only in very recent times did the Telefunken-Platte Company (a dependent of the Siemens concern, once Ultraphon) decide to install Professor Carl Clewing, who had pursued musical and pedagogic studies in the microphone in his own laboratory, to test the tone of records and make experiments.

There were two wireless schools: the Radio Experimental Bureau at the Berlin Academy of Music, and the wireless class at the Klindworth-Scharwenka Conservatory. To the latter we shall return later. The Academy worked with several instruments on the following system. The students had their performances recorded on wax gramophone records, and so were forced to admit their mistakes; or they were set to criticise the pieces played by their fellow students through the loudspeaker. Certain results of these classes were officially transmitted by the German stations. This did not satisfy the requirements of a really systematic examination of the essential basis of the microphone. More valuable than these studies was the invention of several electric musical instruments by an engineer who taught at the Academy, Trautwein by name, especially that to which he gave his name, the 'Trautonium'.

Now, as to the film schools. The tremendously difficult question of the sound-film, which both dramatically and technically presented hitherto unheard-of problems, had, it is well known, at the outset a very detrimental effect on the standard of production, which was almost exclusively inferior as far as taste was concerned. It was therefore no wonder that quarters interested in the artistic aspect of the question mooted a number of plans to probe the causes of these wretched films to their depths. It must be emphasised that all these attempts derived from parties other than the film industry, though the latter had reason enough to undertake them. They were due solely to private initiative, with the object of creating an institute for aspiring and finished artists, where they could adapt

254

their gifts to the novel technique of a new form of art.

Of course, the promoters of the idea included a number of opportunists (to use a mild word) whose services stood in inverse proportion to the fees they demanded. The most striking examples of film schools established in Berlin on wrong principles were furnished by the sound-film school of Döblin, the film-musical department of the Stern Conservatory (this soon died a natural death), and the Reimann School of Arts and Crafts. The only experiment begun with adequate resources was made at the Klindworth-Scharwenka Conservatory, whose director, Robert Robitschek, realised the new possibilities afforded by the microphonic arts, and, in collaboration with Carl Friedrich von Siemens and myself, in the course of two years built up a large group of valuable apparatus according to my plans, which, in the most varied working combinations, provided an 'Institute for Microphone Research'.

In the lay-out of the syllabus, the structure of which may be taken as a model for similar undertakings, *tone* was made the point of departure, with the idea of classing the new forms of art at the very outset both practically and aesthetically as *acoustic arts*, their chief features being the microphone, the amplifier, and the loudspeaker. A second consideration was that of evolving a system of training, which till that time was of course non-existent. Now as it was to be expected that new results would accrue during the course of the syllabus itself, and in the most varied spheres, and as these results were to produce bases for research and scientific data beyond their educational value, it followed that *teaching and research had to go hand in hand.*

The overlapping of the three microphonic arts was also bound to influence the curriculum of the sound-film department. It involved main and subsidiary subjects, which were graded for the various classes of students in such a way that each one of them became acquainted with every subject, and only pursued his main subjects longer and more thoroughly than his subsidiary ones, which in turn were taken by others as their main subjects. In this way the students acquired a complete survey of the total ground: and this is just what they need above all in the sound-film.

The following were catered for: composers, actors, and singers, authors and dramatists, directors, cutters, and sound-technicians; for the latter there were special musical courses. For composers (who interest us most in the framework of this book) there would be three main subjects:

(1) *Composition* (introduction to film music, exercises in silent-film music, theory of beat and dynamics, exercises in film composition, practical studies and demonstrations at the apparatus);

(2) *Instrumentation* (the cinema orchestra from the silent to the sound-film, microphone scores, practice at the microphone and the loudspeaker, microphonic instruments);

(3) *Sound-dramaturgy* (metre and dynamics in the sound-film, music in the dramatic texture of the plot with demonstrations on sound-films and practical experiments at the instruments, sound-perspective, musical dramaturgy).

Their subsidiary subjects would be as follows: dramaturgy, mounting (including both picture and sound cutting), film technique (involving the making of the film strip, studio routine, developing of films, projection), sound-technique (recording, reproduction, acoustics), film finance, laws of copyright and contract, speech and song before the microphone (phonetics).

Correspondingly, a singer would have to complete the following main subjects:

(1) *Training in enunciation and singing* (practice in front of the microphone, voice-records on gelatine and wax discs);

(2) *Dramatic art* (training in expression and body-movement, the art of mimicry and gesture, science of dress and costumes);

(3) *Studio routine* (lighting effects, technique of make-up, camera-focussing).

The subsidiary subjects attached to this course would be the study of dramaturgy and director's technique, as well as all the other subsidiary subjects of the composer's course. We can thus see how the various studies overlap each other and deal fully with every stage of the film in proper gradations. And attached to the main courses we find practical experiments in the sound-film studio, so that the participants in the various courses, after very exact preparation for an experiment in theory, learn how to realise it in a short time in the studio. The short films for experimental purposes which result from the pupils' efforts could possibly be made available for public exhibition.

Exactly similar to the above was the basis on which the curriculum of the wireless department was planned, whereas the students in the gramophone-recording section took part in certain courses in the sound-film and wireless departments, above all, the ever-recurring practical work at the microphone, the loudspeaker, and the unit used to record the discs.

Another new section which would have to be annexed is that for research in the field of microphonic instruments. This scientific department would have to work in conjunction with another established for research into the question of vibration.

The importance of such an Academy for the Microphone need not only consist in artistic and scientific results; for the film industry would be able to save expensive studio rents (by having good work done in advance on their films) and thus cheapen its production. This would certainly be an added factor from the economic point of view. After all, the training of efficient successors to take the place of present-day staff, and the evolution of new technical and artistic forms of the acoustic arts, would likewise redound to the advantage of the industry. This being so, it is doubly regrettable that an industry which has such capital resources at its disposal should nowhere have carried out the idea of financing an Academy for the Microphone. The work of the Institute for Microphone Research in Berlin failed, owing to the changes in the political sphere, which made impossible further work on the part of those chiefly responsible for the functioning of the Academy.

The organisation of such an institute, it is true, requires a considerable capital sum to purchase apparatus, without which any attempt at a microphone school would result in hopeless failure. (For this reason, too, we can assert that the arrangements made in some Paris Conservatories to establish classes in sound-films, wireless, and gramophone recording, separate from one another, are but transient.)

On the model of the Institute for Microphone Research and its principles of 'simultaneous teaching, self-instruction, and research', the following equipment would be required:

(1) Sound-film reproduction unit in its own projection room, and attached to it a playing-desk for records with several turn-tables.
(2) Sound-recording equipment on gelatine and wax; if possible, a steel-ribbon unit of the Stille system (see p. 103), which is ideal for practice purposes and far cheaper than the sound-on-film principle, for example; the incorporation of the latter in such an academy is merely a question of finance.
(3) Listening and cutting station.
(4) Transmission room, and loudspeaker-control room.
(5) Amplifier room, with pre-amplifiers and main amplifiers; microphone couplings, if possible, in every room, as well as reproductive apparatus. Connections in every direction, so that recording and reproduction can take place in all rooms. A good part of the educational success of the scheme depends on this system.

It is a matter of course that close co-operation on the part of the film companies with an institute of this kind should enable the latter to work on a more ambitious scale, and give its students opportunities to carry out their studies on a practical basis. But it should not happen that leading industrial authorities try to restrict the curriculum of the institute.

The establishment of such a Microphone Academy naturally will involve much labour, great experience, and considerable sacrifices of ideal and material resources. But this selfsame experience has taught us that it is altogether senseless to create anything of

260

this sort, unless it is complete in every detail. The country which first succeeds in making a Microphone Institute a reality will certainly reap the benefit of untold advantages of an artistic, scientific, and financial nature: the possibilities of such investigation in relation to the art-forms of the future cannot be foreseen.

It would indeed be highly desirable for the progressive British film industry to decide, in its own interests, on such an institute. It would thereby take the lead once for all in Europe in the artistic advancement of the film. It possesses sufficient space and all facilities in its new and modern studios to carry out the ideas here outlined, The whole scheme would base on a single 'Central Acoustical Institute', which would be responsible for all aspects of sound production, whether artistic, technical, or commercial. The material advantages of both better and cheaper sound would coincide most happily with the ideal benefits accruing from a farsighted artistic policy.

So this demand is not in the nature of visionary illusion. No, it is the outcome of a pressing need, a need which is in the air, and will in the long run prove to be an inevitable development.

Part Six: The Future of the Sound-Film

Part Six

The Future of the Sound-Film

The sound-film is only a few years old, and yet it has already quite a number of the most varied style-periods behind it. It is absolutely impossible to forecast how many yet lie before it! This frequent change in artistic form, which is in pronounced contrast to the constant development of science, is clear proof of the sound-film's efforts to consolidate its position as an art-form, and the little success which has hitherto attended these efforts.

The cardinal error of the first period, which is still evident, lies in the idea that the sound-film is nothing but a substitute for art, a mere mechanisation of traditional arts. As long as the shadow of this idea hangs over it, no further activity can attain an object worth while. The guiding principle for any artistic work in connection with the sound-film must be the conception, as it were, of a *new dimension*, in order that people may at last rid themselves of the idea that it is a substitute for living stagecraft, or just silent film with sound grafted on to it.

265

The future of the sound-film

Does man stand behind the machines? Who is the dominating factor in the mechanical arts? Man, or his machines?

There are two schools of thought which are in complete disagreement over this important question. The descendants of the Romantics wish to represent the machine as merely man's multiplying and recording equipment, and to create living art by mechanical means. They forget that their view leads to tinned musical products, which is certainly not what they have in mind. The other school of thought maintains that man is playing a more and more subordinate part, inasmuch as, though he is qualified to conceive and mould the idea, the execution of it is left to technical resources. According to this view, the handwritten sound-track could well act as a type of what the sound-film of the future will look like.

Now it is an undoubted fact that all this passionate denunciation of machines will not check—at most it may delay—some such development. There are various reasons for this. In the first place, it is only logical that an art so technical as the sound-film should strive to take advantage of every resource which mechanical appliances could possibly grant to it. In the second place, there are weighty reasons of a sociological nature: the gradual decline of those strata of society which have hitherto set the fashion, has put the multitude eager for knowledge, instead of the aristocracy of birth and intellect, in the judg-ment-seat. Aristocratic arts like opera and the con-cert are being pushed more and more into the back-ground: they retire from the stage of to-day, assume the character of museum-pieces, in short, are little else than the privilege of a small proprietary class, which is shrinking with each year that passes.

We know the huge extent to which the film has become the property of the broad masses of the people. It has made itself the popular art *par excel-lence*. It has set in train a mechanisation of art which is now in the ascendant, and this movement is founded on deep causes. It is to-day not too early to assert that the present tendency of society towards collectivism—that is, the abandonment of the indi-vidualism on which the culture of the last century was intrinsically based—is rapidly and most success-fully paving the way to an expansion of this 'mech-anisation' and to the creation of a 'social' art of the future.

Well, it may be asked, what does 'mechanisation' really mean? Not merely the artificial preservation of a work of art by mechanical means. No, it also im-plies, logically enough, a remoulding, in form and in content, of the products of art to be transmitted, ac-cording to the needs of a new social culture and new technical resources. And here it does not matter at all whether the artistic effect is obtained by human or by artificial agency. The final artistic achievement stands once and for all time, because it is anchored in a permanent form, and can always be reproduced at any time in the same quality as when it was first created.

If we proceed to a radical analysis of the facts, we shall find that, accurately put, it is only a question of partial mechanisation, eliminating all the accidents of human performance in art, and thus transcending all personal factors of the present and its variable mental and bodily states. But that need not preclude an enhanced output of works of art. On the contrary, it will mean in all probability a *crescendo* in still more highly finished masterpieces.

We must not overlook the fact that man's productive power remains limited in comparison with that of the machine working under his inspiration. In alliance with the machine, the bounds of film music are almost beyond imagination. Though men could not create *homunculus* by chemical means, they will at least be able to rehabilitate themselves by their achievements in art. Sounds, which one can produce from nothing with the help of science—the possibility of being able to create those sounds in endless variations and make human instrumentalists unnecessary—and, on the other hand, methods of recording, which achieve the most astonishing effects by technical means, although they do but reproduce

268

normal sound-combinations made by human musicians—these are all goals of endeavour which either have already been partly attained, or will be attained in the not too distant future.

Without writing down a single note—for musical notation is a cumbersome device, quite inadequate to register the sound-textures of the future—the composer will present his artistic fancies in a form that will as little correspond to normal spatial dimensions as the film in its visual aspect, whether it be on a plane or possess plastic properties.

But to make this possible—to prevent the evolution of an art-form, so pregnant with future possibilities as the sound-film, being delayed out of all reason—there must first be a complete change in the attitude of film production, especially in relation to film music. For there is surely no vestige of doubt left among both experts and laymen of the film that the present status of the sound-film and of film music is far below the standard set by technical conditions and artistic inspiration. That is solely and without exception the fault of the film's business men, who make a practice of underestimating the public's taste and great thirst for knowledge, who are unwilling to spend a penny on technical and artistic experiments, and who make no attempt whatever to eradicate the last traces of the bad reputation, of which even the sound-film could not entirely rid itself, by more substantial achievements. They do not see that their policy is of ephemeral value and in the long run will be—can only be—prejudicial to their own interests.

It is sometimes said that the necessary reform of the sound-film must start with the scenario. That is only partially correct, for what is lacking is due consideration of the musical factor, without which no manuscript worthy of representation as a sound-film (that is, not merely a stage play converted for film purposes) can possibly be real and vivid at all. The sound-film of the future will, there is no doubt of it, be made much more in the light of music than of the spoken word. And that is why no reform of the sound-film can take place without a reform of film music. Author and composer are like two gangs of workmen boring from two different sides into a mountain, to meet finally in the middle of the tunnel.

If the film's business men will not recognise this fact, all the worse for them. The public will not consent to be their dupe for ever. One day it will have enough of their sham and deceit, enough of their arrest of all the normal development of things. And then cinemas will be empty. Originally educated in bad taste systematically by the whole of world production, people at last are beginning to feel that they must be brought to a better insight and a higher

270

level of culture. For it cannot be emphasised too often that the film seems to be the instrument chosen to take over the succession from the hide-bound traditions of histrionic art.

It is not our intention here to follow blindly those pioneers who are always pushing much too far in advance for the broad masses of the people to be able to follow them. But we must point out that the films, which exercise a daily influence over millions of men and women, are fitted, as no other element in our present-day life, to raise and ennoble the intellectual standard of the masses.

Music, that unique, curious, and psychologically still inexplicable art, has a conspicuous part in the development and the perfection of the sound-film assigned to it. It is intended as the function of this book, to excite the interest of experts and the general public in film music (alas, till now it has been small indeed), and to inspire those who are marked out for it to theoretical and practical co-operation in the future. They would thereby not only be serving the cause of the film to come, but also that of music itself—music, which deepens and enriches the whole meaning of life, and is a symbol of harmony and peace.

THE END

Index